Avril drew a
"She's your daughter..."

Isam stood utterly still. It was only the flare of his nostrils and that rapid pulse at his temple that proved he was alive, not some graven image.

"My daughter? Our daughter?"

Isam might be good with babies but he wasn't in any hurry to accept fatherhood. He shook his head then turned on his heel and crossed to look out onto the dark street.

Be fair. It took you long enough to get over the shock of being pregnant.

Minutes later he swung back. But instead of excitement or the tenderness she'd seen when he looked at the baby, his expression was set, sending a ripple of disquiet through her.

"We'll need a paternity test. I'll arrange it. Someone will come tomorrow."

Now it was Avril who rocked back in shock. When she found her voice it was strident but undercut by a telling wobble. "You don't believe me? You think I'm lying about my *daughter*?"

"It doesn't matter what I think, Avril. I'm a king. Others will need to be convinced. This needs irrefutable proof."

Annie West has devoted her life to an intensive study of charismatic heroes who cause the best kind of trouble for their heroines. As a sideline she researches locations for romance whenever she can, from vibrant cities to desert encampments and fairy-tale castles. Annie lives in eastern Australia with her hero husband, between sandy beaches and gorgeous wine country. She finds writing the perfect excuse to postpone housework. To contact her or join her newsletter, visit annie-west.com.

Books by Annie West

Harlequin Presents

One Night with Her Forgotten Husband
The Desert King Meets His Match
Reclaiming His Runaway Cinderella
Reunited by the Greek's Baby
The Housekeeper and the Brooding Billionaire
Nine Months to Save Their Marriage
His Last-Minute Desert Queen
A Pregnancy Bombshell to Bind Them
Signed, Sealed, Married

Royal Scandals

Pregnant with His Majesty's Heir
Claiming His Virgin Princess

Visit the Author Profile page
at Harlequin.com for more titles.

UNKNOWN ROYAL BABY

ANNIE WEST

PRESENTS

Harlequin®
PRESENTS™

ISBN-13: 978-1-335-93923-4

Unknown Royal Baby

Recycling programs for this product may not exist in your area.

 Harlequin Enterprises ULC
22 Adelaide St. West, 41st Floor
Toronto, Ontario M5H 4E3, Canada
www.Harlequin.com

Printed in Lithuania

MIX
Paper | Supporting responsible forestry
FSC® C021394

UNKNOWN ROYAL BABY

For Jan Van Engen,
who loves sheikh romances.
It's great to know you're waiting for this one.

CHAPTER ONE

HIS HIGHNESS ISAM IBN RAFAT, Crown Prince of Zahdar, rose from the conference table, walking around it to the interviewee. 'Thank you, Mr Drucker. This has been a most useful meeting.'

Avril stifled surprise. As His Highness's assistant, it was her role to usher guests through the presidential suite before and after meetings.

Drucker realised that too. He couldn't mask his excitement as his host personally escorted him from the room. The visitor didn't even spare her a glance, much less say goodbye to her, though they'd had several conversations prior to today and he'd been surreptitiously checking out her breasts through the meeting.

Repressing a fizz of distaste, she focused on her notes.

It was some time before her boss returned. The hotel was one of London's finest and the suite took up a whole floor.

When the door reopened she looked up, skin prickling in the way it always did when Isam was around.

He'd stripped off his suit jacket. Her gaze snagged on broad shoulders and a body that seemed all lean, hard muscle beneath his perfectly tailored shirt and trousers.

She drew in air, trying to slow her racing pulse. Clearly

she wasn't used to being around such masculine perfection! She needed to get out more.

The irony wasn't lost on Avril. She hadn't begrudged her cloistered life and now Cilla's death had given her more freedom. Yet these past weeks she'd had to force herself out of the house. Grief lay heavy and she felt bereft. Cilla had given her stability and love for as long as she could remember. She didn't want freedom at the cost of her great-aunt's life. She missed the feisty, frail, wonderful woman.

Her emotions were all over the place.

That was why she was so unsettled. It wasn't just the impact of being physically near her boss instead of separated by a continent.

He tugged his tie loose and undid two shirt buttons. 'You don't mind, do you, Avril? It's been a long afternoon and I hate being trussed up in a suit.'

But you wear it so well.

She bit down the words. The fact he was even more attractive in person than in his photos was a shock she still grappled with after days working side by side.

It's ridiculous. He pays your salary. You've worked for him for six months.

But her brain had trouble equating this stunningly handsome, charismatic man with the clever, demanding, yet approachable colleague she'd come to know and like via email, texts and phone calls. The man with whom she'd built a rapport, even, to her surprise, a level of friendship.

She was his only UK-based PA, working remotely. She was the conduit for his business interests in Britain while he lived in Zahdar or travelled the globe.

Yet sometimes, when he'd anticipated her next words during a long-distance call, or made her laugh with his wry, insightful humour, she'd felt they understood each other in a way that transcended business. Lately she'd felt closer to him than to anyone other than Cilla.

Avril fought an unfamiliar full-body blush. 'Of course I don't mind, Your High— Isam.'

His dark eyebrow had shot high in a look of mock severity. But when she used his name instead of his title he smiled his approval.

Absolutely, you need to get out more, when a man's smile makes your stomach flutter.

Yet his familiar name tasted strange now on her tongue, though she'd been calling him that for months.

Isam in the flesh was an altogether more sensational being than the faceless colleague to whom she'd grown close.

She'd only ever dealt with him, not any of his other staff. Given the frequency of their communications and the growing understanding between them, he'd insisted on using first names. Avril had been surprised, but what did she know about the ways of royalty?

Yet what had seemed practical and easy when he was far away grew more difficult as they worked together in his private hotel suite.

Because now he's not just your employer. He's the sexiest man you've ever met. The first man ever to awaken those dormant feminine longings.

She hoped he had no idea how he made her feel. It was as if her life of sexual abstinence—because she'd had other responsibilities and no time for a boyfriend—finally took its toll.

She'd never had such vivid sexual fantasies as in the last couple of days, since Isam came to London. Last night she'd lain awake for hours imagining how it would be to touch him, kiss him, undress him.

Even now she couldn't stifle the burr of excitement under her skin at being near him. Or the unfamiliar ache in her pelvis.

Hurriedly she pressed her thighs together.

'That was a useful session, don't you think?' Her voice was stilted and she took refuge in her notes, pretending absorption in what she'd written.

Because she feared what he might see in her eyes. It was vital she remain professional, unswayed by his bone-melting smile.

He flopped into a chair beside her. From the corner of her eye she saw him spin to face her, knees close to her, solid thighs encased in charcoal superfine wool. 'Very useful. What did you think of him?'

'Me?'

She shouldn't be surprised. Isam regularly sought her input. But something in his tone made her look up sharply.

Dark grey eyes regarded her intently. Beneath his imposing, straight nose, his sensuously sculpted mouth had flattened. The angle of his jaw seemed sharper. He looked—not disapproving, but not happy.

What had Drucker said to get Isam offside?

'It's not my decision but—'

'That's never stopped you giving input before.'

Startled, Avril hesitated. Isam might be demanding but he was never impatient. She firmed her lips and lifted her chin. 'I wouldn't employ him.'

Something flared in that gunmetal gaze but she had no hope of identifying it. 'Go on.'

She shrugged. 'On paper the deal seems promising. But I'm not sure he has his priorities right and that doesn't say much for his judgement. He pumped money into creating executive suites in his hotel but I think he's overcapital-

ised. They're underutilised, maybe because of the location. It's the more affordable accommodation that brings
in the money there, yet he refuses to take an interest in
that. Plus…'

A nod encouraged her to continue. 'He skimmed over
the issue of staff underpayment. From what I've been able
to discover that's an ongoing issue. If rumours are to be
believed, it's a major problem. Apart from the legalities,
do you want to take on someone who doesn't value and re-
ward staff? If you acquired the hotel I definitely wouldn't
keep him on as executive manager.'

'I caught him staring at you.'

Discomfort lifted her shoulders. 'Some men seem unable to resist leering at a woman.'

Even an altogether ordinary woman in a plain navy suit
and white shirt. It was something she hadn't missed when
she left her job in an office to work from home remotely
as a virtual PA.

'I apologise that he made you uncomfortable, Avril.
That's why I cut off the meeting. I won't do business with
him. But I needed to meet him and ensure I was making
the right decision.' His tone darkened. 'That short session
convinced me.'

Isam had ended the meeting because his visitor ogled
her? She blinked, digesting the idea. Avril had known there
was something wrong—they hadn't got through half the
points she'd prepared. She slanted a glance at Isam and discovered him watching her with a look of concern.

'It's all right. I—'

'It's *not* all right, as I made clear to him just now. But
thank you for your patience today. I'm sorry it happened.'

He'd called the guy on his behaviour? Avril reminded
herself it was only what any decent person would do. She

should have done it herself instead of pretending it wasn't happening by focusing on her work.

That Isam hadn't ignored the behaviour, but had done something about it, released a flood of warm emotion.

You're not here to feel emotion. You're here to work.

But she couldn't suppress the warm glow inside.

'I'll tidy my notes and send them to you. And the list of action items from today's meetings.'

She paused, reluctant to continue because, despite the long day, and the session with Drucker, she'd enjoyed herself. Enjoyed being with Isam. She liked the way he worked and that he valued her input.

A secret, feminine part of her thrilled at being with this potently masculine, charismatic man.

Plus she hated the idea of returning to the empty house she'd shared with Cilla. Isam was so *alive*, so real and strong. She craved some of that strength and assurance. Craved the excitement of being with him as an antidote to the bleak loneliness of her home.

'Thanks.'

Isam paused, a couple of frown lines appearing on his forehead. Instead of detracting from his handsome features the hint of extra gravity only enhancing his allure.

Careful, Avril. You sound starstruck.

'I fly back to Zahdar tomorrow but there are some things I still need to sort out.' He shot a look at his watch, a sleek statement piece that probably cost as much, if not more than Cilla's house and all the adjoining ones in their terrace. 'It's late, but can you stay back to work this evening?'

Avril stiffened, hesitating. Not because she begrudged him her time. But because working any longer with Isam in his private suite wasn't a good idea. Not because he'd be anything other than professional. But because her feelings about him were increasingly chaotic.

Face it, woman! They're not chaotic. You know exactly what they are. Excitement. Old-fashioned attraction. Lust.

'The hotel does an excellent dinner and my driver would take you safely home afterwards.' Grey eyes narrowed on her. 'Unless you have another engagement?'

Desolation shot through her, undercutting any half-formed idea of excusing herself to avoid an evening closeted with him.

She had no engagements, except watering her great-aunt's African violets and finishing the job she'd begun earlier, sorting Cilla's clothes to donate to charity.

Isam watched Avril's mouth crumple for a second before curving into a smile.

Something in his chest clamped painfully tight.

This smile wasn't like the warm ones she bestowed when caught up in their work and enjoying herself. When she forgot he was a crown prince. It was more like the polite expression she'd worn as she'd ushered Drucker into the room.

Abruptly he sat back in his seat. Surely she didn't equate him with Drucker! Isam might be dangerously drawn to his delightful PA but he'd been careful not to reveal it. Despite the fact that over the months they'd worked together they'd developed an easy familiarity, an ability to anticipate each other's reactions, a rare type of intimacy he'd never known with a woman.

The power imbalance between them, the fact he paid her salary, made it impossible for him to act on his attraction. Avril Rodgers was out of bounds. Even if she didn't work for him, he sensed she was a home and hearth sort of woman, not like his usual sexual partners who were happy to indulge in a short-term affair.

Isam had spent the last four days, since his arrival in London, constantly reminding himself that Avril was a work colleague. The difficulty was that too often he caught her looking at him with definite sexual interest that fed his own desire and weakened his scruples.

When her brown eyes shimmered like old gold and she slicked her bottom lip with her pink tongue, regarding him with a mix of eagerness and awe, she tested every good intention.

But not now. Now, he knew something was wrong, and it evoked every protective instinct.

'Avril, are you okay?'

She blinked, banishing that momentarily haunted look, and sat straighter. Yet her restless hands gave her away. 'Of course. I was just thinking about tonight.'

'It's short notice. I understand that you can't—'

'I can. I'm free tonight. I can stay on.' Her smile this time was more familiar. 'Easier by far if we finish whatever work you have in mind before you leave for Zahdar.'

Isam reminded himself he was a disciplined man. A few more hours in close proximity to temptation wouldn't matter.

Though Avril was like no temptation he could remember. Capable, organised and clever, she was the perfect PA. But there was something else, a warmth, a genuineness, that called to him. Not to mention a sexual allure that frankly stunned him. She wore conservative suits with a minimum of flesh on display, so different from many of the women he met on his travels. But despite her air of wholesomeness…

Better not to think about. Or about how Drucker's lewd appreciation had evoked in Isam something like jealousy.

You want her to look at you, only you.

Who was he kidding? He wanted a whole lot more than Avril's looks. His gaze caught on her capable hands, now neatly clasped in her lap. Too often he'd imagined them on his body.

Isam shot to his feet and strode around the long table, shoving his hands in his trouser pockets in an attempt to hide his burgeoning arousal.

'Excellent. What would you like for dinner?'

Hours later, Avril stretched stiff muscles and rose from her chair. Isam had left the room to take a private call from Zahdar. She'd finish her work. Soon she'd leave.

Would she see Isam again? Probably, but not for a long time. They'd go back to working at a distance.

That was good. She needed that distance.

Yet she wished…

Don't even think about it! You're too sensible to pine for what you can't have. You and he… Inconceivable!

She grabbed her barely touched glass of red wine and stalked across to the window, not bothering to put on the shoes she'd discarded under the desk while they worked.

She'd requested a glass of wine to accompany the superb meal she'd been served, but then hadn't had the stomach for it. It was Cilla, dear Cilla, who'd loved the occasional glass of Shiraz. It must have been sentimentality that made her order the glass.

Avril looked out across the dark street to the leafy park that made this Mayfair location so desirable. It had rained while they worked. The pavements shone, reminding her of the night Cilla died.

Melancholy filled her. She knew Cilla had been in pain. That slipping off peacefully in her sleep had been a blessed release. Cilla had wanted, insisted, Avril not mope. Her great-aunt had even made her create a list of fun things she wanted to do when the time came and Avril had more time for herself.

Her lips twisted. Cilla had been a remarkable lady. She lifted her glass in silent salute and took a long, slow sip, savouring the wine's mellow fruitiness. It warmed her, a comforting glow settling deep inside her.

Tomorrow she'd honour Cilla by reading through that list, though she wasn't in the mood to try new adventures yet.

Unless Isam was on your list. Then you'd be ready for adventure.

'Avril.'

His deep voice came from so close behind her that she jumped, twisting around.

Isam stood there, dark shadows dusting his jaw, making him look even more elementally, bone-meltingly male.

She saw him in the same moment she registered the wave of red wine arc up from the glass that jerked in her hand. In slow motion she saw it collide with his pristine shirt and horror filled her.

Avril put the glass down to search for a tissue but her bag and jacket were at the other end of the imposing room. The dinner napkins had been cleared away long ago.

'Handkerchief? Tissue?' she rapped out.

A large handkerchief, ironed and snowy white, was pressed into her hand. 'Thanks.'

She held it to his shirt, knowing she was probably ruining both, but unable to watch the spill dribble further. With her other hand she tugged open a shirt button then another and another. 'You need to get this off straight away. Salt will lift the wine stain. Or soak it in cold water.'

Beneath her touch she felt the sudden flex of warm muscle. A waft of air eddied across her forehead and she realised it was Isam's breath, soft as a caress.

Avril froze, eyes widening as she realised what she was doing. Her left hand pressed the damp handkerchief to Isam's chest. His hard, hair-roughened, golden-toned chest.

She gulped. The fingers of her right hand were curled, immobile, around a shirt button halfway to his belt.

Only now did she register the rise and fall of his chest with each breath and the friction of chest hair against her knuckles. A tickle of excitement lifted the hair at her nape and pulled her scalp tight.

'I can take it from here.'

There must be something wrong with her hearing. Isam's voice sounded strained, gravelly rather than smooth. The blood pounding in her ears must be to blame.

Her flesh tingled all over and her nipples pushed hard against her bra, making her shiver.

'Of course.'

Her gaze was glued to her hands against his chest but her synapses weren't firing properly. She should be lifting her hands off him yet they didn't move. Her brain was too scrambled. Or her body refused to heed its orders.

She'd dreamt of touching him, of seeing the powerful body beneath the custom-made clothes. The reality was shockingly arousing. Isam in the flesh short-circuited her ability to move.

Two large hands covered hers. But instead of dragging them off him, those long fingers wrapped around hers. Avril's breath disappeared in a gasp.

Sensations shot through her. His scent, citrus and warm male flesh. The gentle strength of his touch. A sudden twitching movement of his pectorals. The quick thud of his heart against her knuckles. As quick as her own, surely.

'Avril. Look at me.'

Reluctant, because she knew this had to end and the fall-out would be embarrassing, she arched her neck, her gaze snagging on the bronzed column of his throat, strong and fascinating. Up to that determined chin, dark with an evening's beard growth. She swallowed hard, taking in the sculpted perfection of his mouth, the long, aristocratic nose, stopping when she reached heavy-lidded eyes.

She jumped and would have tugged her hands away except he held them against his chest.

Because what she saw was unprecedented. Isam's expression was aware. Aroused. Sensual.

All the things she'd believed impossible.

Of its own volition, her body swayed closer, her breasts pressing against his hard torso, stealing her breath from her lungs as his heat engulfed her. Sparks ignited across her skin and her blood shimmered as if effervescent.

Someone's breath hitched. It must be hers, but then she felt the rise of his torso as if he held back the air in his lungs.

Avril couldn't find anything coherent to say. No man had ever looked at her the way Isam did now. As if he wanted to eat her all up. As if he craved her the way she longed for him.

It made her feel different. Powerful.

She swallowed, the movement jerky as though her muscles forgot how to work. Dry-mouthed, she swiped her tongue over her bottom lip.

Heat blazed in Isam's eyes, his nostrils flared, and suddenly he didn't look like the civilised man she knew but some marauder. The glint in his eyes was surely avaricious, and his hands tightened possessively. Avril thrilled at the change in him.

'Isam.'

She had no trouble now, saying his name. It emerged as a whisper, husky with longing. She rose on tiptoe, needing to bridge the gap between them.

Except with shocking finality, he shattered the precious moment. Still gripping her hands, as if knowing her legs were wobbly, Isam stepped back. The room was comfortably airconditioned, yet it felt as though an arctic blast swept between them. Avril shivered.

His voice was deeper than she'd ever heard it, with an accent edging his previously perfect English. 'This can't happen.'

Yet it *was* happening. Didn't he feel it?

'I employ you. You depend on me for your salary.' He shook his head, his mouth crimping down at the corners. 'It would be wrong.'

Avril understood. There was a power imbalance between them. He didn't want to take advantage of her and she admired him for that.

Yet this need wasn't wrong. It wasn't tainted. It was mutual and ferociously real.

More real than the grey half-life she'd been living lately. She *craved* this as a diver, too long below the surface, craved air.

Even now, as she watched him distance himself, the hammer beat of her heart and the jittery restlessness low in her body were all about *her* needs, not something imposed by him.

'Couldn't we pretend that you're not my boss? That I'm not your PA? Just for this evening?'

At any other time she might have winced at the stark

need her words revealed. But this between them was so consuming, it superseded the normal rules. In twenty-six years she'd never experienced anything so visceral.

He scowled and even then she hungrily devoured the sight of him—no longer urbane and in control, but prey to strong emotions, like her. 'No. Absolutely not!'

Suddenly, it was easier than she thought to step away. She wrapped stiff arms around her abruptly chilled body.

What had she been thinking? She'd seen the photos of Isam with a series of stunning women. All glamorous, all beautiful and no doubt at home in his rarefied social milieu. The sort who held down high-flying careers yet found time to look a million dollars at royal events.

'I understand.' Avril struggled not to feel hurt. If she'd thought rationally she'd have known the idea was ludicrous. She didn't fit his world or his expectations. Her stockinged toes curled into the thick, handwoven carpet. 'I'm not sophisticated and sexy and you're—'

'Avril, you've got it wrong.'

She shook her head, pursing her mouth before she blurted out any more foolishness. It was time to leave.

'This *isn't* about you.'

He was trying to soothe her ego but his words had the opposite effect. Her turbulent feelings coalesced into anger, pumping through her bloodstream. She welcomed it because it obliterated, at least for now, embarrassment and disappointment.

'Of course it is. I'm no fool. I know the huge gulf between us. I'm ordinary and you're…you. It was laughable to think—'

'Stop that!' Isam folded his arms, muscles bulging and eyes glinting like molten mercury. He was the image of furious, frustrated masculinity and still he made her knees go weak. But she stood tall and returned his heated stare. 'Do you see me laughing, Avril? I spent today, *all* the days we've worked together, locking my feelings away. Trying to ignore my attraction to you. Pretending to be unaffected and uninterested, when all the time...'

Stunned, she watched a muscle spasm in his cheek as his jaw clenched. The tendons in his throat were taut and she felt tension radiating from him.

He was so angry he *glowered* through slitted eyes.

But instead of dismaying her, his fury had the opposite effect. It told her he felt *something* for her.

She took a half-step towards him. Instantly he pulled back, chin lifting arrogantly. 'That wasn't meant as encouragement, Avril.'

But his hauteur didn't deter her. 'You want me?' The words dropped, soft as petals on dewy grass.

Isam swallowed but said nothing.

'You *want* me!' The realisation eased her racing pulse and soothed the desperate ache just a fraction.

His voice was flinty with authority. 'It would be madness to act on it.'

'Madness, maybe.' She paused to snatch air into oxygen-starved lungs. 'I understand your reservations. Our lives are worlds apart. This can't lead anywhere beyond tonight. You're an honourable man who doesn't want to take advantage.'

Unable to resist any longer, she placed a hand on his arm, feeling the abrupt jerk of muscles in response.

'But what if *I* initiated it? If *I* invited you? It would be a momentary madness and I know it could only last one night. A secret shared by just us.'

She felt a shudder pass from him to her—a quiver of

awareness and deep-seated longing. That proof of connection strengthened her determination. And her recklessness.

'Even if it meant we couldn't work together later, it would be worth it. Don't you feel it too?'

Avril knew instinctively this madness as he called it was what she needed. For the first time in weeks the world made sense in a way it hadn't since she'd lost Cilla. Even if the price was to leave this job, she'd take it. With her skills she'd find work. But where else would she find someone who made her feel the way Isam did?

Even the touch of her hand on his arm was enough to banish the shadows that had eclipsed her life, turning her black and white world into vivid colour again.

Lately everything except work had seemed out of kilter. But this was absolutely right.

Avril needed to feel joy and comfort. She needed the touch of someone warm and living. Not just anyone. Only Isam made her feel this way.

CHAPTER TWO

'OF COURSE I FEEL IT.' Isam's words made her sag in relief. 'But I won't take advantage of you. Besides, I can't offer a relationship, not long term. There are expectations on me that I can't ignore. And I certainly don't want to lose the best PA I've ever had.'

Any other time his compliment on her work would have thrilled her. But Avril had more urgent matters on her mind.

She closed the space between them, standing toe to toe, so her breasts brushed his folded arms as she slid her hands over his solid chest and around his neck. His skin was hot and the sensation of his thick hair against her fingertips elicited a frisson of excitement.

'Then I'll take advantage of you,' she murmured, pulling his head down as she rose on her toes.

Her lips brushed his once, twice, and suddenly he was kissing her back. Powerful arms wrapped around her, pulling her close and high. Against her belly she felt the press of masculine virility and fire exploded in her veins.

Yet Isam's kiss was slow, almost gentle, and totally at odds with her rush of urgent arousal.

Avril leaned in, opening for him, giving kiss for kiss. Still he took his time, as if needing to be sure of her.

She'd never kissed like this. Clumsy Christmas party

pecks and dates with guys who were either too tentative or way too aggressive had made her suspect she wasn't missing much by not dating.

Isam made her realise she'd had no idea how a kiss could be. But how badly she wanted to learn. She wanted to grab life in both hands and experience everything she'd missed.

Her legs were boneless by the time he lifted his head, surveying her through silvered eyes that shimmered with heat. That look alone would have seduced her. Not that she needed seducing. She clung to his shoulders, fingers digging possessively.

He opened his mouth to speak but she forestalled him.

'I'm absolutely sure I want this. I don't care about your position or mine. I don't care about the future.' Not even her job was as necessary as this. She breathed deep, his spicy, lemony scent making her heady. 'I *need* you, Isam.'

For a second he didn't move, didn't make a sound. His proud features looked so tight they might have been sculpted from metal. Then his chest rose mightily, pressing against hers and he shook his head, murmuring something in Arabic she had no hope of understanding.

Before she had time to guess at his response he moved. One second she was standing, stretched taut against him. The next she was cradled in his embrace, held sideways against his torso, his arms supporting her back and legs.

He turned and carried her from the room with long, decisive steps and her heart soared. They weren't heading for the exit but the bedrooms.

'You lay waste to my caution, Avril. To everything except my hunger for you. I tell myself I shouldn't, I can't, but it's no good. I want you desperately.'

His voice was rough, almost unrecognisable, and she lifted her hand to his throat where he swallowed hard. Ten-

derness welled up for this strong man humbled by the same
urgent desire that swamped her.

He paused in the doorway, looking down at her, that fe-
rocious blaze of arousal tempered by something that made
her heart split open in wonder.

'But remember, if you change your mind—'

'I won't.'

She covered his mouth with her palm. She didn't want
to talk.

Isam kissed her hand, then opened his mouth and dragged
his tongue along the centre of her palm and right to the tip
of her middle finger.

Avril shuddered and gasped as heat zinged through her
body. She'd never experienced such an erotic caress. Her
breasts seemed to swell, her nipples peaking hard while
inner muscles squeezed tight.

She quivered, shocked at her response and eager for
more. If she felt this way now, how good would it be when
they finally came together?

She looked up into his assessing stare. Was Isam thinking the same thing? His eyes looked molten hot and she
couldn't keep her thoughts to herself. 'I want you naked.
Now.'

She felt a fillip of delight, seeing his eyes widen. But
better was her satisfaction as he strode through the suite
into a vast, elegantly appointed bedroom.

As soon as she was on her feet she reached for his shirt,
scrabbling at the buttons. Yet Isam was quicker than her. By
the time she tugged his shirt from his trousers her blouse
was unbuttoned and open. He pushed it and her jacket from
her body in one smooth movement that reminded her he'd
done this many times before.

It would make sense to warn him of her inexperience,

but Avril didn't want anything to interrupt this moment, or give him a reason to have any more concerns. Instead she reached for the fastening of his trousers.

What began as a deliberate act became a blur of urgent movement. Soon they were on the bed, gloriously naked, Avril breathless at the amazing sensations of their bodies together. Dimly she registered Isam reach for the bedside table, retrieving a condom.

As if her body weren't stimulated enough, the sight of him rolling it on took her to a whole new level of excitement. He knelt above her, exploring her spreadeagled body with hands and mouth so thoroughly and perfectly that it was mere minutes before an orgasm rushed her.

Avril arched off the bed, responding instinctively to his mouth at her breast and his hand between her legs. The sensations were overwhelming, utterly sublime. Yet as she finally came down from that amazing high, her eyelashes spiked with frustrated tears. She'd had no time to explore his fascinating body, much less have him inside her as she craved.

'Avril, you are you okay?' His voice was a concerned rumble against her ear as he hauled her close.

He wrapped his arms around her as she sank against him, bones melting in ecstasy. His tone grew imperative. 'Tell me. What's wrong?'

She shook her head, her vision blurry as she opened her eyes to meet his worried gaze. 'I couldn't wait. It was incredible.' *He* was incredible, so passionate yet tender. The way he touched her both reverent and carnal. 'But I wanted the first time to be *with* you. Not your hand but...'

A grin cracked his taut expression as he rolled her onto her back, nudging her thighs wide so he could settle between them.

Her already overburdened senses frantically registered new delights. The weight of him, even though he propped himself on his elbows. The incendiary heat and the fascinating hardness of his erection. The tickle of chest hair against her breasts that made her arch and rub her nipples eagerly against him. That felt incredible.

As she moved his breath hissed and his erection pulsed against her, making her eyes widen.

'Is that what you want?' he growled. The timbre of his voice made every fine hair on her body stand up in anticipation.

'You know it is.'

Avril reached down to touch him but he clamped her wrist, pulling it away. 'Better not.'

There was no time to protest because then Isam moved and her world would never be the same again.

Imagination was no preparation for the wonder of them coming together. She'd known the mechanics but reality dumbfounded her. Strange, yes, with a feeling of fullness she couldn't describe. A momentary flinch of pain, quickly gone, obliterated by delight.

It felt as though she'd waited a lifetime for this. The wild beauty of it. The earthy reality of body joining with body. And something more. Something like relief and glory and compulsion all tangled together.

Isam looked so serious, watching her hawk-eyed as he moved slowly, awakening her body to a new reality. But Avril was eager to learn and share the ecstasy he'd already given her. Soon she was moving with him, hands clutching him tight.

His gaze flickered when she hitched her heel around his muscled thigh. Instinctively she'd wanted to lock them closer together, only to discover the new angle heightened her pleasure. He helped her hook her other leg around him.

Isam paused, teeth bared, nostrils flaring, a man on the edge.

He looked...untamed. And she revelled in the change from urbane businessman to elemental lover.

This was how she needed him.

With gritted teeth he withdrew then bucked his hips, driving her to a new, extraordinary height.

After that there was no more slow. The control he'd so obviously exerted crumpled under a rush of sensual need. They moved together, gasping, hearts racing, and Avril felt a rush of pleasure gathering again in her pelvis, her breasts, her blood. Until her vision started to splinter as ecstasy engulfed her.

She opened her lips to call his name just as he claimed her mouth and their striving bodies hit the summit together.

The world spun out of control as light burst behind her eyelids. There was only Isam, holding her tight as he lost himself in her, introducing her to paradise.

Later, much later, when she could conjure the energy, Avril smiled and pressed her mouth to his damp skin, rejoicing in his tiny shudder of reaction and the murmur of satisfaction that rumbled from his chest into her body.

Life was good. So very, very good.

Get out of bed. Do it now.

Through the curtains no one had bothered to draw last night, the faintest morning light was visible.

Isam had an early flight to Zahdar that he couldn't miss. Before that he wanted to see Avril home.

Avril, who'd tempted him beyond reason, beyond the limits of his control, into reaching out and taking what he wanted. He'd *known* he shouldn't, known that, despite her eagerness, there'd be complications, and *still* his vaunted self-control had proved no match for his hunger. That was a first.

Never had it occurred to him that she'd be an innocent.

A shiver skated through him as he remembered the moment when he'd encountered that fragile, unexpected barrier and her honey-brown eyes had widened in consternation that turned quickly into pleasure.

Isam told himself that if he'd known he'd never have taken her to bed. Bad enough that he'd broken every rule by sleeping with someone dependent on him for her salary. But to take her innocence too...

In front of him Avril stretched in her sleep then burrowed back against him with a little twitch of her *derrière* that brought her flush against his erection. Involuntarily his fingers closed harder around her soft breast and his chest grew weighted as his lungs tightened.

Get out of bed. Do it now.

While he still could. Before she woke. It would be better if he were up and dressed by then because it would be easier to resist her. To talk sensibly about the implications of what they'd done.

Yet he couldn't bring himself to move.

Unfamiliar emotions eddied in his belly. Even when he'd discovered her lack of experience he'd been unable to rein in his desperate hunger. He remembered the final ecstasy of their joining, her clutching tight as he bucked hard and fast. Too hard? Too fast? She'd climaxed. She'd looked adorably sated and smug afterwards but had he hurt her?

Isam wasn't used to such ambiguities around a lover. He wasn't used to questioning his actions.

But you've never had a lover like Avril.

Even before they'd had sex, something about Avril set her apart from other women. Why?

She wriggled again in her sleep, this time arching so her breast thrust into his cupped hand. A spike of heat shot to his already tight groin.

His eyes rolled back and he gritted his molars at how very good that felt.

Everything about her felt good, which was why he'd broken another of his rules and spent the whole night with her.

Usually Isam slept alone, even after sex. He'd learnt years ago that it helped remind lovers that what they shared was mutual pleasure only, not commitment. He wasn't ready for a long-term partner, not yet. For when he did, that partner would become his wife. It was what his country expected of him.

Now he'd spent the whole night with a woman. Not any woman but his PA, who, unbelievably, had been a virgin.

What was wrong with men in Britain that no one had tempted her into bed before?

Even as he thought it, he winced at the idea of Avril sharing herself with some other man.

He bent his head a fraction and nuzzled her hair. Last night it had been a revelation when he'd seen it loose for the first time. Thick and long enough to cover her breasts, it was a sensual curtain that only heightened her seductiveness.

He breathed deep, inhaling her honey scent. Not sugary sweet but like the rich dark honey from the mountains of Zahdar, full-flavoured and lusciously addictive.

Addictive is the word. You need to get up now and—

'You *are* awake.' Her husky, morning voice was a caress, making his erection pulse against her. 'Oh!'

Was that an 'oh' of dismay? Or delight?

Isam lifted his hand from her breast and drew away. Only to have her roll over and fix him with a searching stare.

Desperately he tried not to notice all the delicious curves on display. He swallowed hard and kept his attention on her face. She was flushed, a crease down one cheek from how she'd lain on the pillow, and her hair was rumpled. She looked so delectable he had to curl his hands into fists rather than reach for her. Pain scored his palms.

'You *don't* want to have sex with me again?'

Her mouth turned down in a delicious pout.

When had Avril learned to pout? At work she was all professional decorum. The way her lips thrust out was damned near irresistible.

'I see.' The pout disappeared and her expression grew sombre. 'Of course. I wasn't thinking. It's time I left so you can—'

He grasped her shoulder as she rolled away, turning her back to face him. 'Wait.'

It didn't matter that he'd been telling himself it was time to get up. He didn't like it when she wouldn't meet his eyes.

'It's okay. I understand. I wasn't meant to stay so long.'

The fact her words echoed his own thoughts only made him feel worse. Because, whatever this was, Avril wasn't like any of his previous lovers.

You know what this is. It's a minefield. A potential disaster. Sleeping with your PA! You've never behaved so appallingly.

Yet Isam couldn't bring himself to regret what he'd done.

That, more than anything, should have raised a red flag. But he was too busy reading Avril's dull flush and her unhappy expression.

He kept his voice soft. 'Why do you think that?'

Her mouth turned down. 'Because you're a prince. And I'm…' She paused so long he wondered if she'd continue. 'Me. Ordinary. Last night was a mistake.'

She reached for the sheet as if to cover herself but he was lying half across it and refused to move, because inexplicably her words fired his anger. She'd merely stated the obvious, but he didn't like it. Didn't like her calling herself ordinary. Avril was many things but not that. As for her assuming last night was a mistake…

It didn't matter that he'd thought the same himself. To hear her label it that was insupportable. He didn't stop to question why.

'Do you really think last night was a mistake, Avril?'

Her expression changed. Her jaw set and she met his gaze squarely. 'No. It was wonderful. The most amazing thing I've ever done. But I understand that for you it's problematic, sleeping with staff. Inconvenient. Maybe even embarrassing.'

He knew she was trying to be pragmatic, yet the words felt like a slap to his face. Even though he'd been torn between berating himself over his behaviour and revelling in the memory.

'You're not an embarrassment, Avril. And you're definitely not an inconvenience. Last night was unfortunate because I overstepped the boundaries—'

'Unfortunate!'

'But I can't regret it. I can't wish it undone.'

He watched her process that, understanding dawning.

During meetings she was the consummate professional, no sign of her emotions. But now he read her like a book. First hurt at believing herself rejected, then regret, then finally annoyance. Now suspicion mixed with something that made her eyes shimmer.

'If you don't regret it, why pull away from me just now? Is it that after last night, you're just not interested any more?'

He felt his forehead twist into a scowl that she should even think him uninterested. He was about to counter with a reference to his painful erection but stopped.

She couldn't know what was going on in his head.

'I know years ago the press painted me as a bit of a Casanova, but I was never as bad as they made out. I'm not so callow.'

Besides, after one taste of Avril how could he conceivably have lost interest?

Only the truth would do.

'I spent the night alternately dreaming about you and awake, fantasising about having you again.' He watched her eyes grow round. 'But I thought you needed your rest so I resisted waking you. Especially in light of your inexperience.'

Isam waited for her to say something about that. To explain why she hadn't warned him, though he suspected she'd feared, rightly, that he'd stop.

Such confidence in your self-control. You were in such a lather, chances are you wouldn't have been able to hold back even if you'd known.

'You wanted me...after?'

'I did, do.' He saw the spark of excitement in her gaze and felt compelled to go on. 'You're right, we've created a complicated situation—'

Her voice was breathless. 'You want me.'

There it was again, that satisfied smile he'd found so bewitching last night. Isam couldn't help but respond to it. His facial muscles stretched in a grin that he knew was more lascivious than circumspect.

Because suddenly, despite the caution he should employ, despite a lifetime learning to put royal responsibilities and expectations before everything else, he couldn't dwell on the complications they'd created. He was just a man, bewitched by an alluring woman. A woman watching him with wonder and excitement.

Blood rushed to his groin, leaving him light-headed.

'I want you,' he admitted again and felt the last shackles of restraint fall away.

'I'm glad.'

That was all it took. Her sweet smile, her shining eyes and her welcoming smile. All thought of protocol, duty and the world beyond this bed became hazy and insubstantial.

Isam stroked her cheek with his knuckle, watching her voluptuous shiver that made her berry-tipped breasts shake invitingly. Then slowly, because, despite the thrumming urgency of his need, this was too important to rush, he gathered her to him.

CHAPTER THREE

One year later

'THIS WAY, MS RODGERS.'

The tall man in the sharp suit gestured for her to precede him into the hotel's lift. His smile was perfunctory, not reaching his eyes. He had an air about him that made her wonder if he was a bodyguard, not an administrative assistant.

His stare made her shiver and pull her too-snug jacket close, the hairs at her nape rising. Would he frisk her before she was allowed into the presence of His High-and-Mightiness?

She didn't relish the thought. But she'd see this through. Now she had a chance to confront Isam.

Her emotions were a chaotic jumble and her stomach churned with something close to nausea. Avril had never believed today would come. After a year of complete silence, he wanted to see her.

She'd almost, *almost* refused to attend.

She'd stomped around the house, muttering under her breath about self-centred men and their unconscionable behaviour. The message, not from Isam himself, but from an officious staffer she didn't know, had caught her by surprise. To her horror, she'd found herself blinking back furious tears, bombarded by relief, anger and disbelief.

Not excitement. She'd given up on that ages ago.

How could she be excited to see him again? She'd almost convinced herself that the thrill she'd felt that night with him was her mind exaggerating. He'd been her first lover and, for a while at least, she'd turned him into someone special, more admirable than the flawed, arrogant bastard he'd proved to be.

Her breath caught on a bubble of bitter laughter that felt scarily hysterical. No, he wasn't a bastard. Not as far as the world was concerned. Not long after leaving London, on his father's death, he'd moved from being the legitimate royal heir to being proclaimed King of Zahdar.

But handsome is as handsome does, as Cilla used to say.

He'd treated Avril appallingly. She'd never be able to respect him after what he'd done.

'Are you all right, Ms Rodgers?'

Her gaze snapped up to the man she was sure now was a minder. Did Isam fear she might physically attack him? Unlikely, since she'd be no match for him. More likely royal security was more obvious now he was Sheikh.

'Oh, I'm just dandy. Thank you.'

She watched her companion blink and realised her smile held a feral edge. Drawing a slow breath, she forced herself to be calm or at least to look it.

The lift bell pinged and the doors slid open to reveal the elegant opulence of the presidential suite's foyer.

In the almost thirteen months since *that* night, Avril had never ventured back here. Isam hadn't returned but stayed in Zahdar since commencing his reign.

Because of her?

Unlikely. It was clear the man she'd thought she knew

didn't exist. She'd fallen for a mirage. She'd invested Isam with a character that matched his outwardly attractive appearance. Now she had the real measure of the man. Not admirable. Not attractive. Not worth pining over.

Avril smoothed her hand down the russet fabric of her straight skirt. It wasn't new, she wasn't going to waste her money on a new outfit for this meeting. But it was a favourite, even if the fit wasn't quite as it used to be, and it made her feel good.

'Thank you,' she murmured as the minder led her into the suite then opened the door to the conference room.

She stepped over the threshold and heard the door snick closed behind her. On the other side of the table sat three men in suits. She only had eyes for the tall one in the centre.

Her heart took up a rackety beat, pounding her ribs as she met clear, pale eyes. Something like an electric charge jolted through her. Despite being prepared for this meeting, moisture tickled her hairline and bloomed across her palms, making her tighten her grip on her laptop case.

He stared straight back at her and her peripheral vision dimmed as her focus narrowed to eyes the colour of a grey winter's morning. Eyes that scrutinised but gave nothing away. Eyes that didn't flicker with even the tiniest hint of pleasure or welcome.

Avril *thought* she'd been prepared, thought Isam couldn't hurt her any more, but that unresponsive stare pierced the armour she'd spent so long constructing.

She put her palm to the centre of her chest, trying to hold in sharp stabbing pain.

'Ms Rodgers? Ms Rodgers.' She turned stiff neck muscles to find a man beside her. He was in his forties, with a round face that looked more suited to smiling than the frown he wore now. He wore a bespoke suit and concern in his eyes. 'Please, won't you take a seat?'

Looking from him to the empty seat beside the Sheikh, she realised he'd come around the long table to her. How long had she stood there, aware of nothing but Isam?

'Thank you.'

She sat as he introduced himself and the man still seated next to Isam. But she didn't retain their names, too frantically focusing on trying not to show how badly shocked she felt.

'And you know Sheikh Isam,' he added.

Belatedly she realised she hadn't remembered the obligatory curtsey for Zahdar's head of state. Not that the man deserved a curtsey.

Avril inclined her head. 'Yes, we've met.'

Was it imagination or was there a ripple of reaction to that? No, not a ripple. More a sudden stillness, as if her words put them all on alert.

Probably imagination. She made an effort to get a grip. There, that was better. A slow breath out as she clasped the arms of her leather chair. She was in control of herself now. The worst moment was over.

They'd seated her on the opposite side of the table. As if for an interview. Did they think to intimidate her with formality?

Her attention returned to Isam, directly opposite. He leaned sideways as his companion murmured something. Without his steely gaze on her she scanned his features, stunned at the changes in him and even more at how familiar he was. Her fingers twitched as if remembering the smooth flesh of his back and rounded buttocks, or clutching at his thick, surprisingly soft hair as they kissed.

His cheekbones were the same, sharply defined with angles a camera, or a besotted woman, would love. His mouth was pursed rather than relaxed and his nostrils flared as if something annoyed him.

But what caught her attention were the deep grooves carved around his mouth. The lines at his eyes hinted now at pain rather than pleasure. And of course the scars. A web of them at one side of his brow, extending up into his hairline.

Simmering anger disappeared, replaced by dismay. She'd known he was injured in the helicopter crash that killed his father soon after Isam's return to Zahdar. But seeing the evidence brought a sharp, iron taste to her tongue.

It took a moment to realise she'd bitten her lip in distress.

When the accident happened she'd been frantic with worry. The Zahdari press had provided little insight into his condition. Every press release from the palace had seemed designed to obfuscate.

But eventually there'd been good news. Reports of the new Sheikh out of hospital, recuperating privately. Then of him taking up the reins of government. Then a few photo opportunities showing him at a distance, usually consulting with elders or opening some new facility.

Abruptly Isam turned and she felt the force of his stare like an assault. It seemed to drive right into her, probing and analysing. Threatening to shatter the hard-fought-for equilibrium she'd finally achieved.

What did he want from her?

'Thank you for coming today, Ms Rodgers.' It was the man with the round face and glasses who spoke. 'His Majesty is reviewing his interests in the UK, hence today's meeting.'

Did you really expect him to come here to take up

where you left off that night? To see how you were? If you were okay?

Pursing her lips, she inclined her head. She'd known this would be a business meeting.

She still had to work out how she could get time alone with Isam. Despite her deep-seated disgust at his behaviour, there were things she needed to say. Things that weren't for the ears of strangers.

'If you don't mind, we'll start with your position.'

Avril started. Her position? Her gaze darted to Isam's but his steady stare was blank. She breathed deep.

She lifted her chin. Two could play at being aloof. 'What do you want to know?'

She kept her focus on Isam but again it was the man beside him who spoke. 'Your role, for a start.'

That wrenched her attention to him. 'I'm His Majesty's PA in the United Kingdom.'

'His Majesty hasn't given you any instructions for some time. Yet you continue to draw a salary.'

It was the thin man on Isam's other side who spoke, the one who looked as if he'd swallowed a lemon. He made it sound like an accusation, as if Avril had done something wrong, stealing from the royal coffers instead of struggling to manage responsibilities beyond her remit because her boss had lost interest in his enterprises here and cut off communication.

Her hackles rose. It certainly wasn't her fault!

'I'm afraid that's something you need to take up with His Majesty, not me.' She turned to skewer Isam with a glare that should have pinned his worthless hide to his chair.

'Since his last visit I've managed as best I can. I was given clear parameters about regular auditing of and reporting from his UK enterprises. There are quite of few of them.' And not all had been happy at the lack of direct contact from Isam, leaving her to handle their expectations when she herself didn't know what to expect. 'You'll find full updates and progress reports in my regular emails.'

As well as her desperate appeals for him to contact her. All of which remained unanswered. Her chest rose on a shuddering breath but she sat straight, shoulders back and chin up.

Still Isam said nothing, yet she saw a flash of something in his expression that told her he wasn't as cool as he appeared. Good! He deserved to squirm, ignoring her calls and emails. Presumably, too, informing his staff not to accept any call she made to the palace.

She'd spent too long and given up too much of her pride trying to contact him. She wasn't in the mood to put up with any more nonsense.

'As you say, a series of emails, yes.' The first interviewer looked down at his notes. When he lifted his head his smile was easy yet instinct told her he hid something. 'And the email address you sent it to? I'm afraid I didn't have time to make myself a copy of the relevant reports before the meeting.'

Avril frowned, darting a look at Isam, but he was in whispered conversation with the other man. This was beyond odd. Why let his staff question her about her job rather than focusing on the work that badly needed his attention?

She spelled out the email address, watching as it was written down. 'If there's anything in particular you need to see, I can show you now.'

She put her laptop on the table and watched three pairs of eyes swivel to look.

'Your work device?' asked the thin man with the dour

expression. At her nod he continued. 'Excellent. If you could call up the most recent report that would be useful.'

Avril did as requested, but, instead of asking questions, the thin man walked around the table and with murmured thanks took the laptop back to his seat.

Startled, she looked at Isam for explanation. Didn't he trust her any more?

He didn't look quite so detached now. Long fingers massaged his temple, making her wonder if he had a headache, and as their eyes met she saw something that might be regret.

As if! She was the one who'd learnt about regret. And that her instincts were severely flawed around this man.

The first interviewer interrupted her thoughts. 'Now, Ms Rodgers, perhaps you'd like to tell me about your work history, your skills?'

'Sorry?'

'I'm interested in why you applied for the position and what you brought to it.'

Indignation rose as a premonition rippled down her spine. They were going to sack her?

Avril didn't mind that. She no longer wanted to work for Isam ibn Rafat. She should have resigned long ago instead of holding out that secret hope that he'd finally contact her and they'd talk. But she'd not allow them to imply it was because of the standard of her work.

She turned to the man she'd once esteemed. More than esteemed. 'Isam.' Protocol be damned. 'Do you want to tell me what this is about?'

In her peripheral vision she saw his minders stare at her use of his personal name. It was probably an offence back in Zahdar. The dour man's jaw actually dropped and the other one darted a wide-eyed look at his sheikh.

Her boss, her one-time lover, took his time responding and every second felt like a new betrayal.

'I know this seems unnecessary, given that you've worked for me for some time. But we're bringing my UK interests in line with my other investments. That means a detailed review of current arrangements.'

It was the first time Avril had heard his voice in over a year and she was shocked by how it affected her. Deep and smooth, with just a hint of huskiness, it trawled through her, snagging on sensitive spots, drawing a flurry of excited response.

Her hands tightened around the chair's armrests and her thighs clamped together in instinctive rejection of that lush softening at the entrance to her body.

How could her body betray her after the way he'd treated her? He'd used then ignored her as if she were nothing.

'Rashid here—' he nodded to the man with glasses '—oversees all palace staff. Before I became Sheikh I preferred to manage my British investments personally rather than through Zahdar's public service. But now, as Sheikh, it makes sense to draw it all together under one umbrella.'

He lifted those broad shoulders in a shrug that should have made his statement reassuring, as if the review were a trifle, but the movement was stiff. Did he still carry injuries from the crash?

Avril jerked her thoughts back. Isam would have the world's best specialists attending him. She needed to concentrate on what this meant for her position.

Avril had told herself that cutting ties with Isam was the only way forward, though it meant finding a new position when she least felt up to it. But to be chucked out on the pretence of not doing her job, just because he was embarrassed by her presence, was beyond the pale.

'So you're rationalising and looking to sack me?'

That, at last, drew a reaction from Isam. He leaned towards her, horizontal lines grooving his forehead. 'I didn't come with any such intention. This is an information-gathering session only.'

He seemed so earnest, so persuasive, she was tempted to believe him.

Until she remembered the man who'd left her over a year ago with a promise to return in two weeks. She'd understood when he didn't. The crash that injured him and killed his father had made international headlines. So she'd waited, hoping, fearing and praying for his recovery.

And then…nothing. Not a call, not an email, not a response to any of her messages. His phone was unanswered and palace staff had been polite yet dismissive when she'd called the switchboard.

'Perhaps it would be easiest if we started with how your previous work fitted you for your current position.'

At Rashid's words she reluctantly turned to him. 'I can supply my résumé if necessary. I worked my way up through a series of positions until I was personal assistant to Berthold Keller.'

That grabbed her audience's attention. Rashid's eyes widened. 'The property magnate?'

'That's him.'

'But you must be no more than in your mid-twenties. That's a very senior position at a young age.'

She'd turned twenty-seven a few months ago. 'I'm pleased to say my previous employer valued competence over seniority.'

She spared Isam a sideways glance, challenging him to

comment, but of course he said nothing. At least this session was destroying the last of her silly yearning for a man who'd only existed in her imaginings.

'I'm very good at what I do.'

Cilla had said she had an old head on young shoulders. She was organised and hard-working, with an eye for detail, traits learned from her great-aunt, along with the desire to be financially independent.

'So why did you leave?'

'Working for Mr Keller involved a lot of travel, which was stimulating, but over time I realised I wanted to stay in London.' Because Cilla, her feisty, independent great-aunt, had grown physically fragile. 'It was Mr Keller who recommended me to the Sheikh.'

In response to Rashid's questioning look, Isam nodded. 'He's a friend. I respect his judgement.'

Then he rose, resting his palm on the gleaming wood as if for support. But any thought that his injuries had weakened him physically were banished as he straightened to stand tall and imposing. There was no weakness in this man just as there was no softness.

It had been her mistake ever to imagine such a thing.

Even so, Avril's pulse spurred in anticipation of his invitation to follow her for a private conversation.

'If you'll excuse me…' his gaze swept the three of them '…there's something I must do. I'm confident you'll make good progress without me.'

His gaze met hers for the briefest of seconds. This time it wasn't blankly disinterested. His eyes looked stormy and she could almost imagine a bolt of lightning tearing through the room. She shivered in response to some unseen reverberation.

Then, to her astonishment, Isam left without a backward glance. As if she held no more interest for him.

CHAPTER FOUR

ISAM STRODE THROUGH the suite, his steps growing longer and faster. The straitjacket binding his shoulders and upper arms tightened and the talons ripping through his gut sharpened, threatening to shred his self-control.

Finally he reached the sanctuary of his room.

His head throbbed with a familiar ache that he'd learned to despise. It was the reminder of all he lacked. Of the weakness he hid from all but a trusted few.

But he didn't reach for pain relief. Instead he sank into a tall wingchair, leaning his head back against the upholstery and squeezing his eyes shut.

Instead of darkness he saw grey, shot through with snatches of light. They were fragments, like a shattered window pane, separate and useless.

Like you.

He firmed his jaw. No, not useless. Just not as he was.

A bitter laugh rumbled up from his chest but he didn't let it escape. He couldn't allow self-pity.

Besides, what had he to feel sorry about? He was alive and almost whole. Whereas his father...

Isam breathed through the racking pain of loss that still, sometimes, seemed too great to bear.

Easier by far, and necessary, to concentrate on the problem that was Avril Rodgers.

The disjointed pattern in his mind's eye transformed into a woman. Thick brown hair swept up behind her head in a businesslike bun. Businesslike, too, her court shoes and skirt suit.

But there'd been nothing businesslike in the way he noticed her. The tight fit of her rust-coloured jacket over her breasts. The purity of skin that he imagined to be as soft as the petal of a creamy rose. The restrained yet unmissably feminine sway of her body as she crossed the room.

Even the smudges of tiredness under her eyes made her controlled professionalism seemed gallant, as if weariness would never interfere with her ability to do her job or stand up for herself.

He swallowed hard, knowing she was different. *Feeling* it in every pore of his body. Despite a natural masculine tendency to notice an attractive woman, he didn't usually react so viscerally.

The radiance of her brown eyes, warmed by glints of gold, made him think of welcoming firelight on a chill desert night. The way her lips pouted when she was annoyed and the flash of hauteur, when she thought her competence questioned, intrigued and invited.

He couldn't prevent a snort of laughter. She'd looked daggers at him. There was no invitation there.

But that hadn't stopped his reaction.

His pulse accelerated as broken images teased him.

The curve where her neck met her shoulder. His nostrils flared on the scent of aroused woman and wild honey and his lips tingled at the brush of velvet-soft skin.

The flare of shock in warm brown eyes, accompanied by a whispered gasp, before she relaxed against him, her eyelids dropping to half-mast in a sultry look of invitation as her body welcomed him.

A ruched, dark pink nipple cresting a breast so perfect the sight of it dried his mouth. The feel of her breast, just the right size for his hand that trembled as he cupped such beauty.

Isam's eyes snapped open as blood surged into his groin. How long since any woman had made him so weak with desire, so quickly?

He'd come to London knowing he had issues to resolve. Things he had to deal with before he could continue to give his full focus to his country. It had been a challenging year. All Zahdar mourned his father and looked to Isam for reassurance, while he still struggled with his loss. This had been one of the most difficult times of his life.

Yet beyond all the urgent demands on his time there had been a niggling urge to set aside his duties and the worries of a nation, and come to London. Of course he'd put his people first and remained at home. He understood they'd feared he might die from his injuries too.

But now you're here, what next?

One look at Avril Rodgers had told him this wouldn't be easy. She'd been left to her own devices for over a year, a situation that needed to be rectified immediately.

But he couldn't concentrate on office arrangements and communication protocols. Not when she bombarded his brain with sensual impressions that sent it into overload.

In the early days after the accident there'd been times when concentration was difficult. When he'd felt his mind fight for focus. When brain fog had been a constant barrier to progress. He'd been told not to worry, that he *would* improve. But to a man used to decisiveness, proud of his mental agility and focus, that had been far worse than the various breaks, bruises and lacerations.

Avril threatened that focus more than he'd imagined possible. Alarmingly so.

There was no way Rashid and his staff could fix that. Isam had to do that for himself. Alone.

The doorbell rang after dusk and Avril rolled her eyes. Would this day ever end?

She'd gone to Isam's hotel sure that at least she'd have the satisfaction of telling him what she thought of him. But the coward had walked away, leaving her to defend her work and her character to his minions.

Then, as soon as she'd walked in the door hours ago she'd been run off her feet. She hadn't even had time to change out of her office clothes, simply stepping out of her shoes and promising herself a long soak in the bath later, if she could keep her eyes open.

Though, given her indignation at how today's meeting had played out, she suspected sleep wouldn't come easily tonight.

She stifled a yawn as she walked to the front door, then, realising who it must be, she smiled as she opened it. 'Gus, it's lovely—'

Her words died as she registered, not the comfortable round outline of her neighbour, Augusta, but a towering form, all hard, masculine angles. She'd know those shoulders anywhere and the proud angle of that head.

Without even thinking about it she swung the heavy door forward. Instinct was a skittering creature racing up her spine, whispering in her ear that having that man in her home would be disastrous.

The door juddered to a stop. She pushed but it wouldn't

budge. Looking down, she saw a large, glossy shoe wedged in the doorway. She hoped his foot was bruised.

'I don't want you in my home.'

From beyond the door a deep voice said, 'You'd rather we had this conversation on the doorstep? For the entertainment of your neighbours?'

Avril opened her mouth to say her neighbours were lovely, unlike him, then snapped it shut.

'Or shall we have this out in my suite? Perhaps over the conference table with Rashid taking notes?'

She yanked the door open so hard it almost bounced off the wall beside her.

'Don't you come here with your threats. You think you're a big man, high-ranking and powerful. But there are more important things in life. Respect, for one.' She jammed her hands on her hips and seared him with her scorn. 'Common decency.'

She was so incensed at his nerve in coming to her house after effectively dismissing her earlier, she could barely catch her breath. *That* was why her breathing was so choppy, her breasts rising so vigorously they tested the buttons of her blouse.

Avril crossed her arms over her chest.

'We need to talk.' Something in his tone quelled her surge of anger. He didn't sound smug, but strained. 'We both know it.'

Finally she nodded. 'We do. Tomorrow. I'll meet you somewhere.' Somewhere neutral like a coffee shop. 'What time—?'

'Not tomorrow. Now.' When she didn't respond, merely lifted her eyebrows in a show of disdain, he continued. 'My time in London is limited. Most of it is accounted for. If we want a private discussion it needs to be now.'

'Surely a king can set his own timetable.'

He merely shook his head slowly as if to say she had no idea of his schedule.

And he'd be right. What did she know of royal life? The few days she'd spent with him had been remarkable for their informality.

Informality! Hysterical laughter at the understatement threatened her composure.

Avril had sudden recall of how it had felt when he'd taken her to bliss with his body, then held her close, whispering words of affection. Even now the deep timbre of his voice made something loosen inside her.

She'd wanted to see him for so long. Been desperate to see him. Now here he was and it was like a nightmare. Nothing was as she'd once hoped. Even her determination to despise him was undercut by her body's response to his nearness.

'Avril?' Her gaze lifted to his and was trapped. His eyes gleamed pewter-dark. Did she imagine they looked troubled? 'Let me in.'

Reluctantly she stepped aside and he walked past, so close her skin prickled and she closed her eyes in momentary despair. She loathed this man. He'd treated her badly. Yet her yearning body hadn't yet got the message. But after tonight she'd probably never see him. One way or another she wouldn't work for Isam after this.

'To the left.'

She followed him in to see him standing, surveying the old-fashioned furniture. The packed bookcases and clutter of photos. The thought of him snooping through her life, hers and Cilla's, made her step forward to stand in front of the display.

'Take a seat.' Because she'd feel better if he weren't dominating the room with his height.

But it wasn't just his height. He'd always had an energy about him, a charisma she'd never been able to ignore.

To her relief he sank into a large armchair, looking just as at home as he did at that dauntingly large conference table.

Or naked in bed. His musculature and that fine dusting of hair across his chest utterly fascinating.

Appalled at her thoughts, Avril took a chair opposite him. She didn't offer refreshments. This wasn't a social occasion. Just as well Cilla wasn't here. She'd been a stickler for polite niceties.

'Why are you here?'

'I thought that would be obvious. To talk about us.'

'There *is* no us! You made that clear when you refused to answer my calls and messages.'

A flicker of emotion crossed his face but she couldn't pin it down. He looked down at his hands, triangled in front of him with fingertips touching.

'You tried to contact me.'

It wasn't a question but a statement. Yet there was something about his tone that made her hesitate for a second. But she wasn't in the mood to play games. They both knew how he'd treated her.

'Of course I tried to contact you. Even if I didn't have work issues to discuss, I was worried.' At least at first. 'Your crash made world headlines. But no one seemed to know how badly injured you really were.'

Grey eyes lifted and met hers. 'As you see, I'm fine.'

He didn't look fine, she realised with a shock of clarity that made her insides twist. He looked…gaunt, as if a sculptor had chiselled his features but gone too far, accentuating deep chasms and angles and not leaving enough flesh on the bone. In the conference room she hadn't noticed, too caught up in her own emotions.

'I'm sorry about your father.'

She knew what grief was like. At least her great-aunt had reached a venerable age and her decline had given them both time to prepare. It must be terrible to lose a loved one so suddenly.

'Thank you.' He nodded. 'He was a good man and I miss him.'

For a moment they regarded each other and Avril could have sworn she felt the ebb and flow of understanding between them.

No. No. No! Don't start fantasising now. He's not that man.

It was time to remind them both that she had his measure.

'I emailed you, multiple times. I called but got no answer. When you didn't contact me, even when you were out of hospital and taking up your duties again, I called both the Zahdari Embassy here and then your palace, leaving messages.'

The memory of those fraught months reinvigorated her indignation and hurt. She hadn't expected long-term commitment as a result of the night they'd shared. She was no blind romantic. But he'd made it clear he wanted to see her again.

He'd acted as if he cared about her.

More fool you.

'And I didn't get in touch.' He rested his forehead on his hand, his elbow on the arm of the chair. 'I'm sorry, Avril. I—' He looked up, frowning. 'What's that?'

The sound began low and soft, like the warning hint of

thunder in the distance, making her sit up, dismay filling her. She knew from experience the storm would break all too soon.

She jumped to her feet. 'Excuse me. There's something I need to see to. I won't be long.' She hoped. 'Wait here.'

It was only as she hurried from the room that she realised she was in stockinged feet and wisps of hair hung around her face. It would have been nice to meet him looking cool instead of frazzled. But her appearance was the least of her worries. Her heart hammered desperately.

She stumbled up the stairs, weariness vying with shock. For, after months knocking her head against a brick wall, trying to contact Isam, she'd learnt she was better off without him. Today had just consolidated that, convincing her he didn't need to know about this.

This was her business, not his.

Given the way he'd discarded her without a second thought, without even the courtesy of a call, she'd never trust him with anything so valuable.

The decibels rose as she reached the landing at the top of the stairs and dived into the first room, closing the door behind her.

A couple of minutes later, arms full, she turned at the sound of the door opening, her heart leaping into her throat.

There was Isam, looking ridiculously splendid in his tailored suit and impeccable silk tie, his shoulders almost brushing the sides of the narrow doorway. He looked as out of place in her little home as she would in a palace.

His eyes rounded as he took her in. Swiftly he surveyed the room, taking in the recent changes she'd made, then returned to the weight in her arms.

'You have a baby?'

Her arms tightened around Maryam as she swayed and jiggled, trying to persuade her to go back to sleep.

'Evidently.'

Now he looked more than surprised. He looked stunned. 'It's yours?'

Avril had thought of this moment for so long. She'd imagined so many different scenarios. But now it came to it, the words stuck in her mouth. Her emotions were still so up and down. Half the time she didn't know if her daughter was a glorious blessing or a test she'd fail, despite her best efforts.

She nodded jerkily and lifted the baby higher in her arms, patting her back.

But Maryam refused to be soothed, her grizzles becoming a full-blown cry that made perspiration bead Avril's nape and her stomach churn. She'd spent ages getting the little one settled to sleep. Was it going to be another bad night like last night?

She turned to pace the room. The warm bundle in her arms was familiar now after almost four months, and she loved her daughter dearly, but she was incredibly aware of her lack of experience as a mother.

She'd never been around young children. Never had younger siblings or cousins. She'd been brought up by an elderly woman whose friends were, in the main, old. Avril had never babysat before she came home from hospital with this precious, fascinating, demanding bundle.

Gus, next door, was a fountain of useful information and practical help. Occasionally she'd pop around in the evening with a hot meal she'd cooked, offering to keep an eye on Maryam while Avril ate. For Avril's daughter had the unerring ability to wake, crying, just when her mother sat down to eat or take a bath. As for sleeping...

Avril turned to find Isam had moved into the room, making the nursery smaller than ever.

'You should leave. I'll meet you tomorrow. You'll just have to find time for me in your schedule.'

Was he even listening? His whole attention was on the baby. Avril's breathing snared. Was he noticing her mink-brown hair, so dark it looked almost black? Or her grey eyes?

Avril's arms tightened reflexively and Maryam wailed.

'Is she teething?'

Avril frowned. 'You know about babies?'

He lifted one shoulder, his attention still on her daughter. 'A bit.'

Once more Avril swung away, swaying Maryam and trying to soothe her. Without success. And when she turned there was Isam, frowning. Judging her for not being able to calm her child?

'I don't think she is. And it's not hunger,' Avril explained. 'I just fed her and she doesn't need changing.'

Grey eyes lifted to meet hers and fleetingly it felt as though understanding passed between them. 'Sometimes I think they just want company.'

She felt like saying Maryam had her company all the time. Today had been the first time she'd left her daughter, which had only added to the stress of that formal meeting. Gus had assured her that Maryam had been 'as good as gold' in her absence, leaving Avril wishing she could be a bit more content with her own mother.

'You look done in,' he murmured. 'Why don't you sit down and I'll hold her for a bit?'

She couldn't have been more astonished. But Isam's expression was serious and his tone gentle.

Too gentle. It was easier to feel competent and in control without what looked and sounded like sympathy.

His mouth lifted at one corner in a crooked smile that made her insides squeeze. 'It's a long time since I held a baby.'

He *wanted* to hold her squalling daughter? Or was he just being kind?

Of course he's being kind. But why?

'How long has it been?'

His smile stiffened but he stepped closer. 'My sister was eleven years younger than me.'

Was. Of course, she'd read when researching for her job that he'd had a sibling, but hadn't paid much attention. Now she glimpsed something in Isam's face that made her ashamed not to have registered how much losing his sister must have meant to him.

Spurred by emotions she didn't stop to consider, Avril let him lift her daughter from her arms. As soon as she saw his confident hold and the way Maryam, surprised by the newcomer, stared up at him, something eased inside Avril. Her knees loosened and she sank abruptly into the cushioned rocking chair that she'd brought upstairs for feeding time.

Maryam frowned up at him and he bent his head, all his attention on her. It was strange, seeing them so close together.

Her tiny daughter and this big man who sheltered her so easily against his broad chest. The sight of his protective stance and his absorption made Avril feel strange.

When Maryam waved a tiny hand in the air he offered his finger for her to clutch, and that strange feeling burst into something stronger. A fierce melting, a drawing sensation through Avril's belly, while her heart stuttered before picking up a quickened beat.

She was so lost in her thoughts it took a while to register that her daughter was no longer crying. And that Isam was crooning something she couldn't understand. The baritone rumble of it tunnelled through her body, making taut muscles loosen and easing her jittery tension.

Her brain told her to get up and take care of Maryam herself. But she was exhausted. Would it really hurt to sit quietly just for a few minutes?

How long she sat there, she didn't know. His lullaby worked on her too. She felt her bones melt into the upholstery as she relaxed properly for the first time in what seemed ages. It was only as he moved towards the cot that her drowsy eyelids lifted.

She said nothing as he put the baby down. Maryam's long dark lashes curled across perfect cheeks and her rosebud mouth made her look like an angel. A rush of maternal emotion sideswiped Avril, making her blink and get up to fuss with the blanket until Isam moved away.

Neither spoke until they were downstairs.

'How did you do that?' she asked as they entered the front room.

Avril had lost count of the number of times she'd sung lullabies and walked the floor with her daughter.

He shrugged. 'Maybe I was just different enough to distract her until she dropped off.'

Avril had a feeling it wasn't that simple. Again she wondered about her own competence. Maybe Maryam had picked up on her stress despite her best efforts at seeming calm.

Or maybe you're beating yourself up over nothing.

'What's her name?'

Warily, Avril pursed her lips. But after what he'd just done she owed him this at least. 'Maryam.'

He stiffened, his eyes narrowing. 'That's an Arabic name.'
'Is it?'

You know it is. But you could mention it's used in other languages too.

'You didn't know?'

He paused, waiting for her answer, his gaze searching.

Now the moment had come she wasn't sure she could go through with it. For a year she'd been determined to share this, but today she'd convinced herself that discretion was better. For her daughter and herself.

Yet after seeing him upstairs…

Isam shoved his hands in his trouser pockets, the movement pulling open his jacket to reveal a wet spot on his pristine shirt. Drool from where he'd snuggled her daughter close.

'Avril, you haven't answered me.'

She wrapped her arms around her middle. 'I knew. I looked it up. I like the name but I also wanted something that worked in both English and Arabic.'

He said nothing but his eyes silvered as he stared at her, and she saw his pulse thrum hard.

She drew a sustaining breath. 'She's your daughter.'

He stood utterly still. It was only the flare of his nostrils and that rapid pulse at his temple that proved he was alive, not some graven image.

'My daughter? Our daughter?'

'She was born thirty-nine weeks after you left London.' His head jerked back as if in denial or belated shock. But surely he'd begun to guess upstairs. 'She's ours. Conceived the night before you flew to Zahdar.'

Isam might be good with babies but he wasn't in any hurry to accept fatherhood. He shook his head then turned on his heel and crossed to look out onto the dark street.

Be fair. It took you long enough to get over the shock of being pregnant.

Minutes later he swung back. But instead of excitement or the tenderness she'd seen when he looked at the baby, his expression was set, sending a ripple of disquiet through her.

'We'll need a paternity test. I'll arrange it. Someone will come tomorrow.'

Now it was Avril who rocked back in shock. When she found her voice it was strident but undercut by a telling wobble. 'You don't believe me? You think I'm lying about my *daughter*?'

'It doesn't matter what I think, Avril. I'm a king. Others will need to be convinced. This needs irrefutable proof.'

This. As if her beloved daughter were a *thing* not a person.

She unwound her arms from around her middle. Barely she resisted the urge to walk across and slap him for his unfeeling arrogance. Instead she planted her palms on her hips, feeling the strength of righteous indignation and a rush of adrenaline flow in her bloodstream.

'I don't care that you're a king. I don't want anything from you. Ever.' She moved close enough to make sure he read the fury in her eyes. 'Now get out of my house. I never want to see you again.'

CHAPTER FIVE

IN THE END it was easier the next day to agree to the paternity test than fight it.

Because despite her anger and her hurt that Isam refused to believe her, Avril knew Maryam deserved to have proof of her paternity. Especially since he seemed determined to deny it. Plus it required only a simple cheek swab, no needles.

But what really convinced Avril was the visitor who arrived that morning. A grey-haired woman with one of the kindest smiles she'd ever seen. She said she'd been hired through an agency to provide any assistance Avril required, cooking, cleaning, shopping or helping with the baby.

Avril was in the process of sending her away, hating Isam's presumption that she couldn't manage, when her visitor's wide smile dimmed. She confessed she was finding her recent retirement boring and had leapt at the chance to put her skills to use. She missed being around people, especially babies.

Somehow Avril ended up with a sheaf of recommendations in her hand and a résumé that indicated Bethany had been an early childhood educator before retiring.

A couple of phone calls later, Avril had reassured herself the woman was genuine. By which time Bethany had brought her a mug of tea and a slice of the home-made fruitcake she'd brought. The rich flavour was so like that of Cilla's home baking, it had Avril blinking back tears.

By the end of the day, which included a nap from which Avril woke feeling more refreshed than she had in ages, Avril and Bethany had bonded. The older woman wasn't bossy or judgemental. She had an easy confidence around Maryam and a caring nature. Her reassurance that Avril was doing well, adapting to a new baby, even eased some of her niggling anxiety.

Isam might not want to take an active role in his daughter's life, but something good had come out of his guilt. Avril would accept Bethany's assistance while she could.

She suspected she and Maryam would thrive with the older woman's assistance, which was important. Especially as Avril needed to start looking for a new job. She had money to tide her over for a while after she left her current position, but the sooner she started looking, the better.

She had so much on her mind she could almost have ignored the fact that Isam didn't contact her that day.

When she'd told him to leave the night before he'd surveyed her for what seemed an age, then turned and walked out into the night, leaving her stricken and trembling with an excess of emotion.

Avril hadn't believed he'd go so easily. But he'd probably been desperate to escape the complications she and Maryam represented. She had no idea how children born outside marriage were treated in his country, but suspected a monarch fathering a child by a foreigner wouldn't be generally approved. Royals were cautious about bloodlines and as a new king he'd be particularly eager to avoid scandal.

Maybe he was planning a dynastic marriage. Probably she and her daughter were an inconvenient embarrassment.

She got through the rest of the day trying and failing not to think about the man with the piercing eyes and tight, angular features that made her wonder how much he'd suffered after that crash.

But the night after Bethany arrived, Avril slept long and deep, and for once Maryam wasn't as restless as usual.

Yet when Avril woke, it was to realise she'd dreamt of Isam. Not the rigid man who'd retreated from his child, then left without a backward glance. But the man she'd fallen more than a little in love with last year. The man who embodied an irresistible combination of tenderness and masculine power. Her skin was damp and there was a twisting ache deep in her pelvis as she shoved the bedclothes back and got up.

Later that day Avril was updating her résumé while Bethany looked after Maryam upstairs, when the doorbell rang.

Isam stood tall and imposing but she noticed the dark shadows in his eyes and tension—or was it pain?—grooved around his mouth.

Avril refused to worry about him. He had a kingdom full of people to do that. Instead she folded her arms and stood her ground. 'What brings you back? We've nothing more to say.'

Someone would send the results of the test, and Avril had decided to accept his guilt gift of temporary mother's help.

His jaw clenched but his tone was disarmingly gentle as he said, 'I'm sorry you feel that way, but we have to talk. For Maryam's sake as much as anything else.'

For a minute longer Avril stood unmoving before reluctantly stepping aside. He was right. For Maryam's sake they had to set some parameters for the future.

She led the way into the front room, feeling the atmosphere change from slightly cluttered comfort to sparking awareness as he followed her in. Once again they sat opposite each other.

'The test result is in.'

'So quickly?' She shook her head. 'Of course, being royal you could pull strings. And so? If you're going to tell me it proved you're Maryam's father, don't bother. I already know. I was a virgin before we got together.'

Something flared in the gunmetal grey of his eyes. It looked like surprise. Yet her innocence must have been obvious to him that night. She'd been enthusiastic but not adept.

'I'll have a copy of that report please.' She held her hand out. 'I want Maryam to have proof, since you're so keen on denying her.'

'Denying her?'

How could he deny his own child? Why would he even want to? He knew how precious life was and how easily it could be snatched away.

Isam's chest tightened at the thought of anything happening to his tiny daughter. When he'd held her he'd felt a rush of emotion so powerful it had strained his self-control to relinquish her into the cot and walk away.

One look and he'd suspected her identity. Even the shock of that suspicion hadn't diminished his sense of wonder.

The feel of her in his arms, the way she looked, even that clean baby smell, forcefully reminded him of holding Nur all those years ago. The uprush of emotion had almost cracked his composure. But years of training as Crown Prince had come to his aid, enabling him to hide his wonder, excitement and yearning. And the grief that welled at the memory of Nur.

Suddenly, he had family once more. His mother had died when Nur was born. So when his sister, and more recently his father died, there was only him.

He'd been grappling with so much this past year that he hadn't allowed himself to dwell on that, though grief for his father was a constant. But now he was no longer alone.

'Isn't that what you're doing? A paternity test is hardly the action of a man wanting to accept his child. It's what men do to try wriggling out of their responsibilities.'

Avril folded her arms, the action drawing her T-shirt tight across her breasts and making his palms tingle as if wanting to reach out...

'Don't worry, as far as I'm concerned you won't have any responsibilities. I've learnt the sort of man you are. I'll raise my daughter alone.'

He met Avril's accusing stare and realised she was serious.

The sort of man you are.

Bitterness twisted his lips. That was the sixty-four-million-dollar question, wasn't it? What sort of man was he?

Once Isam had never thought that in doubt. He was honest and hard-working. He had a sense of humour and enjoyed time with friends, especially adventuring on desert trips or kayaking, though he didn't have much free time. He'd spent recent years working with his father for the betterment of his country, though mainly behind the scenes while he managed his own business too. His father had had more patience for the restrictions of royal protocol that Isam found so constricting.

But since the accident Isam's character and abilities had been called into question. Not outright. No one would dare. But the arrangements made to govern the country while he was incapacitated had given some a taste for regal power they hadn't wanted to relinquish. Nevertheless, it was disappointing to know there'd been a whispering campaign against him emanating from that direction.

So easy to blame others. But given your...continuing problem, can you be completely sure of yourself?

Isam refused to acknowledge the poisonous voice in his head. It only came on the darkest days, which, thankfully, were growing fewer.

One step at a time.

'A paternity test is also the action of a sensible man in a position of power.' He refused to apologise for that. It was the reality of his life. 'You must realise it was a reasonable precaution. It doesn't mean I'm rejecting our daughter.'

He saw Avril's eyes grow wide at his emphasis on the word *our*. She swallowed and he guessed that behind her bravado she was scared.

Who could blame her? The stakes were high and they were all but strangers to each other.

'Maryam is *ours*,' he reiterated. 'Not simply yours, not simply mine.'

'So the real issue was that you didn't believe me. You had to make sure I wasn't lying.' Her expression betrayed disappointment and hurt rather than anger, and Isam felt it like a gut punch, driving hard enough it threatened to wind him. The depth of his reaction surprised him. 'What did I ever do to make you think me a liar, Isam? We worked together for months. We had a good relationship. I thought you knew me.'

'Sex isn't the same as knowing someone. Our affair—'

'I wasn't talking about *sex*.'

She interrupted as no one else did, her tone dismissive.

At home everyone was conscious of his royal status. Trying to have a discussion with Avril Rodgers could be

frustrating but he preferred her honest emotion to blind sub-
servience. Or those who paid lip service to respect while
manoeuvring against him.

She went on. 'I'm talking about the way we worked together. You respected me then. You liked me too. I didn't
imagine that. We shared a camaraderie.' Her mouth firmed.
'And I'd hardly call the other an affair.'

The other?

She sounded scornful, as if she hadn't enjoyed sex with
him. Despite the gravity of the current situation, which far
outweighed whatever carnal joy they'd had, Isam bristled.
No woman had ever found him an unsatisfactory lover.

'What would you call it, then, if not an affair?'

She couldn't have thought he was offering a permanent
relationship! Even foreigners understood that a king's bride
had to meet a whole slew of requirements.

It would be disastrous for a royal sheikh to marry a
woman who wasn't up to the job.

His wife would be more than his companion and lover.
She'd be Queen of Zahdar. She'd help him in his work to
support their people and keep their country thriving, with
the best prospects for the future. She'd be in the public eye
every day, a role model to many.

Avril made a dismissive gesture. 'I'd call it a one-night
stand. What else?'

Isam heard the words but instantly rejected them. He
jerked back in his seat, pulse chaotic and thoughts whirring.

'A one-night stand?'

He felt his eyes bulge. Saw her say something but couldn't
make it out over the hammer of his pulse in his ears.

The edge of his vision misted, blurring into grey. But he
saw her, every line and curve clearly defined.

She spoke again and this time he caught the words. 'I

said, what else would you call it? We were only together for one night.'

A one-night stand!

With his personal assistant.

A woman dependent on him for employment and a reference.

A virgin.

A terrible, crawling sensation began in his belly, slithering all over him, making his flesh shrink against his bones.

What sort of man was he?

It seemed people had been right to question after all.

He shot to his feet, paced the small room, then paced back again, unable to sit still. Emotions thrashed through him, needing an outlet.

He swung around again and there was Avril, blocking his way. When she spoke her voice was softer. 'Isam. What is it? I don't understand.'

Nor did he. If anyone had told him he was a man who'd seduce an innocent then dump her after one night, he'd have been insulted. He'd have claimed it was impossible.

Maryam, their daughter, proved him wrong.

He clutched his head, pain flaring at the effort to dredge up the proof that it wasn't true.

'Isam! You're worrying me. Come and sit before you fall down.'

'I'm not going to fall,' he muttered. 'I'm in peak physical fitness.'

His rehabilitation regime had been taxing. Determined to recuperate quickly, he'd pushed himself even harder. He'd always been fit and now he was stronger physically than ever before.

'You're swaying on your feet. Your face has gone grey.'

She half led, half pushed him into a chair. Despite the

adrenaline rush in his blood, he felt as if his bones melted into the welcoming upholstery. He trembled all over.

Shock. More than shock. He sometimes got this heady feeling when he pushed too hard. But not usually this bad.

Soft fingers touched his and he snapped his eyes open, surprised to find he'd shut them.

Avril was crouched before him, curling his fingers around a glass of water. 'Sip it slowly and don't move. I'll be back. I'm calling a doctor.'

'No doctor!'

Her jaw angled pugnaciously. 'You're obviously not well.' When he didn't reply she added, 'I don't want the hassle of a diplomatic incident. Imagine the complications if a head of state collapsed in my home.'

Her pragmatism gave him the jolt of normality he needed. He sipped the water and forced his mind to go blank, as blank as possible in the circumstances. When that didn't work he focused on his breathing. Soon he had himself under control.

'My apologies. I know what's wrong and I don't need a doctor. I didn't mean to scare you.'

He saw he'd done just that. Avril's expression was tense and she was still squatting before him, so near he felt he could lose himself in those golden brown eyes.

She rose but stayed close as if worried he'd stand up. 'You scared the life out of me. Are you unwell?'

'Not unwell.' Technically.

'And? You went as white as a sheet, then grey when I re-minded you we'd only had one night together.' She paused, eyes narrowing. 'You looked...stunned.'

Isam knew he should divert the conversation in another direction. He'd become adept at that in the last months.

But something stopped him. Her genuine fear when she

thought he was ill? Or the memory, the one that had kept him awake last night, of touching velvet-soft skin and hearing Avril sigh in pleasure?

Suddenly he felt exhausted at the need to keep his secret.

'How could you be stunned? You know it for a fact.'

He didn't answer. But he wondered what she saw in his expression for her eyes widened and her jaw dropped.

'Isam? I don't like that blank look. It's as if you're looking but not seeing.'

He was seeing, all right, but not enough. He drew a shuddering breath and gave her the truth. 'I take your word for the fact we just had one night. I'm afraid I don't remember. I have amnesia.'

CHAPTER SIX

ISAM WATCHED HER stumble back a step, eyes round with shock. 'Amnesia? That's...' Slowly she shook her head. 'Do people really get that? I thought it was only in movies.'

A bitter laugh cracked open Isam's tight lips. 'I wish.' How *much* he wished it only occurred in fiction. 'Unfortunately, I'm living proof it's real.'

'You mean, you don't remember *anything*?'

He hesitated. Very few people knew the full truth about his condition. Given his position as ruler of Zahdar, it was thought best to keep the situation confidential. The last thing his people needed was to lose confidence in him. The potential damage to investment, to the massive development projects he and his father had initiated, even potentially to the peace of his nation, was too great.

But already he and Avril shared a potentially inflammatory secret, their daughter. He had to trust her. Besides, instinct urged that she wouldn't betray him.

But can you trust your instincts? Maybe even the memories you do have are flawed and your image of yourself distorted.

That was what some would have him believe. But Isam couldn't allow himself to think that way. He *had* to believe in himself, and now, in Avril.

'I have lots of memories. It's only what happened in the six months or so before the chopper crash that are foggy.'

Foggy. That's a nice euphemism. Why not admit it's basically a great, yawning gap?

'And I don't remember the crash or its immediate aftermath.'

The doctors said it was because of the blow to his head, but the emotional trauma of losing his father to such catastrophic injuries was partly responsible.

Apparently, despite Isam's own injuries, he'd managed to pull his father and the pilot from the chopper before help arrived, though they were probably dead on impact. He'd heard a whispered comment that the scene was one of the most devastating even the seasoned rescuers had ever seen.

Avril stumbled back and sank into a chintz armchair. It was a relief to focus on her. 'The six months before the crash? Does that mean you don't remember...?'

'I remember some things. But even what I do remember, I can't always trust. I've been told that some of my recollections aren't correct.'

His distant relative Hafiz had acted as regent while he'd been in hospital, and some of Hafiz's comments about Isam's actions prior to the accident disturbed him. Made him question what he knew of himself.

It was frustrating and undermined his ability to move forward as he wished. Increasingly he had suspicions about that, but for now he had more pressing matters to deal with.

Avril. And their daughter.

'What *do* you remember from that time?'

He met her eyes and knew what she was wondering. How much he remembered about *her.*

'Not nearly enough. I remember snippets, scenes rather

than complete memories. The visit of another head of state to Zahdar. A friend's wedding.'

He paused, reluctant even now to admit it, but knowing it was unavoidable. 'But not you, Avril. I don't remember you.'

It was a lie. Since seeing her in the boardroom yesterday he'd been getting short flashbacks. Not of any conversation but rather sensual recollections. The honey taste of her on his tongue. The music of her soft cries as she tipped over the edge into bliss. The feel of her body welcoming his.

But were they true memories or wish fulfilment?

Because from the moment she'd walked into the presidential suite yesterday, he'd felt a sensual tug, a deep-seated hunger for this woman who was to all intents and purposes a stranger.

Was it any wonder he'd slept badly?

Isam saw her absorb that, hurt swiftly replacing shock in her expressive eyes.

'You don't remember *anything* about me? You employed me about six months before your accident. We worked together in London the week before.'

Guilt tightened his flesh, making it prickle in discomfort.

How must it be for a woman who'd given her virginity to him, *who'd borne his child*, to discover he had no recollection of her?

Even though he hadn't let her down deliberately, it must feel like a second betrayal, after he'd failed to return to her in London.

It was inconceivable that he could be responsible for the torment he saw in her wide eyes. Yet he knew, with a heavy heart, that it was so.

Isam wished he could make this easier for her. But lying would do no one any good.

'I'm sorry. I don't remember. But when I saw you yesterday you seemed…familiar.'

The fact that he'd been instantly plagued by sensual snapshots had made it impossible to concentrate on the meeting. Snapshots, sensations, yearnings. They had seemed real. Seemed like genuine memories, but could he be sure? And were they of her as he believed? Or of some previous lover?

Racking his overtaxed brain, he'd been unable to recall any lover who matched those memories.

Avril collapsed back in her chair, deflated. 'That's why you were so brusque?' She frowned, her voice dropping as if she spoke to herself more than him. 'That didn't seem natural. It didn't seem like *you*, to blank me like that. You were never a cruel man.'

He was relieved to hear that. Some of the things Hafiz had said lately made him wonder if his view of himself was flawed.

'But your London investments. You must remember those.'

Isam shrugged. 'Only the long-term ones like the hotel where I'm staying. I inherited that from my English grandmother years ago.'

'When you hired me you were in the process of acquiring some British investments. That's why you wanted an assistant in the UK.'

'So I gather. But I don't recall them.'

For long moments she regarded him silently then shook her head. 'Even so, your staff must have known about them. They must have known about me. It's a long time since your accident but I haven't heard a word from you.'

Her stare was accusing, as if she either didn't believe

in his memory loss or thought he'd used it as a convenient excuse to avoid her.

Exhaustion hammered him and he rubbed his temple where the shadow of that familiar ache threatened anew.

'I'm sorry, Avril. I know this seems far-fetched.'

Almost as far-fetched as discovering he had a lover he'd forgotten and a baby. He drew a deep breath.

'It seems you had a personal number for me, not one that was used by my staff. I lost that phone in the crash. The same with my email, I didn't use a palace address. The royal staff weren't involved in my British investments and it seems I channelled that work through you alone.'

Her eyebrows shot up. 'Is that usual? For them not to know anything? I know I only had dealings with you but I'd assumed...'

What could he say? That he didn't know? That he could only guess?

'These UK investments are quite separate from everything else and clearly I'd decided to manage them on my own, with you on the ground here. I wasn't investing public funds. I was using my own private capital, so there is no question of impropriety.'

'I wasn't suggesting that—'

'Of course not.'

But he remained on edge at even a hint of suspicion, Hafiz's innuendos that his priorities weren't always for the public good fresh in his mind.

'That's why your staff were so eager to access my laptop? You really didn't have backup?'

'Of course I have. I just don't seem to have made a note of where. It's not in the cloud storage used for palace records, but then these weren't public service documents. Remember, too, that everyone's focus after the accident was on continuing the usual business of government after so much disruption. There was no reason to look for additional matters off the official books.'

If it weren't so appalling it would be laughable. A king who couldn't even retrieve his own business documents. Because he'd deliberately not wanted to involve the usual channels in these projects.

The few senior palace staff who knew the situation had been utterly discreet, because there'd been enough public anxiety following the crash that killed his father and injured him. For a while there'd been some doubt about how quickly he'd recover. Informing his people that their new king had a faulty memory would hardly inspire confidence.

If word got out about any of this it would be more ammunition for Hafiz, who seemed intent on undermining him.

All Isam knew for sure was that he'd been determined to pursue these investments as separate from any others he owned. He thought he knew why but 'thought' was a far cry from 'knew'.

'So…' Avril drew the word out '…you didn't come to London for *me*. You came to find out about the business.'

He inclined his head. 'I came across a note that made me curious.'

He'd been trying to fill the gaps in his memory, trying to recreate his movements, but his diary had merely said 'London'. Until he'd unearthed a handwritten note with her details, perhaps from when he'd employed her.

'I had my staff investigate and they discovered you'd attended meetings with me.'

They'd also discovered he'd been paying her regularly for some time, which had made even his loyal administrator, Rashid, look askance, until they discovered they were salary payments, all above board, just not organised through the usual channels.

Her tone was sharp. 'You investigated me?'

'Not in detail.' If they had, he'd have known in advance about Maryam. 'I wanted to speak to you myself, rather than rely on others.'

Since being injured he preferred not to take reports at face value. He needed to assure himself that he understood the situations with which he dealt.

A bubble of mirthless humour expanded in his chest. His daughter and his ex-lover were far more than just a 'situation'. They changed everything. For himself and for his nation.

'We need to talk about Maryam.'

In other circumstances he might have waited to bring the conversation around to her. He was conscious that Avril still grappled with the news of his memory loss. He knew the feeling. Every day it was a challenge. And now he'd learned he had a daughter! Not even a year trying to acclimatise to the massive holes in his memory had prepared him for that.

The accident had taken his father from him, robbed him of his memory, and the chance to be there for Maryam's birth. The chance, too, to know her mother better.

But self-pity and time were luxuries he couldn't afford. He needed to protect Avril and Maryam. Their situation left them vulnerable and he couldn't allow that.

They also potentially provided Hafiz with ammunition to undermine Isam's rule. His relative had come to covet the power he'd wielded while Isam was in hospital, but his focus was personal aggrandisement, not the nation's well-being.

Avril didn't look happy. 'I thought you wanted to dis-own her, but now I understand your caution.'

He told himself not to take it personally. She was still grappling with their extraordinary situation.

One thing at least he could clarify. 'I would never, under any circumstances, disown my child. I know what a precious gift she is. I intend to cherish her and give her the best life I can.'

He'd look after her as he hadn't been able to look after Nur. His failure then was still a raw wound after all these years.

But instead of calming Avril's anxieties, his words made her frown. 'You make it sound like *you'll* be raising her. She has a mother, remember.'

Isam looked at the woman who'd been at the centre of his waking thoughts and even his dreams since their meeting yesterday. It was amazing how much she'd got under his skin. But then that shouldn't surprise him, now he knew he'd broken every self-imposed rule by sleeping with her. Whatever he'd felt for her a year ago had obviously been significant. Compelling.

'Don't worry, Avril. I'm fully conscious that you come as a pair. My amnesia encompasses past events only.'

Even now he could barely believe he'd forgotten this woman. The way his body responded to her, the way she drew his gaze and his thoughts...

Exactly what had been their relationship? How had they come together? He was desperate to know, but that would have to wait.

'I'm just trying to reassure you that I intend to be involved in Maryam's life and do all I can to support her, and you.'

Avril stiffened. 'You think I'm looking for a handout?'

'Anything but.' He'd been told she initially hadn't wanted to accept the assistant he'd arranged. Seeing the shadows of fatigue beneath her fine eyes, he was relieved she'd changed her mind. 'I can see you're proud and independent. It must have been taxing, being alone through your whole pregnancy, and now with a baby.'

Had she been alone? He didn't know her family situation. As for her hooking up with another man since their night together…everything in him rejected the idea. That mightn't be proof but he couldn't believe it of her.

How do you know when you can't remember her properly? Maybe Hafiz is right and the injury to your brain is worse than you want to believe.

Another idea Isam refused to countenance.

'I wish I'd known and been able to support you.'

'I…' She sank back in her seat like a woman overcome by the barrage of shocks she'd received. 'Thank you, Isam.'

He clenched his hands around the arms of his chair, resisting the impulse to rise and gather her close. To offer comfort. But he couldn't. Whatever their relationship had once been, she'd given no indication she'd welcome his embrace, even a purely platonic one.

But your response to her is anything but platonic.

Another complicating factor in an already fiendishly difficult situation.

'We still need to talk about Maryam.'

Instantly her chin shot up defensively. Then she nodded. 'Yes. I'm sorry. I'm still getting used to…' she waved a hand in his direction '…the truth about you. I thought you'd deliberately cut me off.'

'There's no need for apologies.' He paused, not wanting to press the point but knowing it was imperative they move swiftly. 'Obviously we have a lot to discuss and I don't want to overload you today. You've had a lot to process.'

And you don't want to scare her by declaring your intentions out loud.

For there was only one solution he could see to this situation. Marriage.

It didn't matter that his country expected him to choose a bride familiar with Zahdar, its customs and language. A bride with some experience of a royal court and the pressures and expectations that would be placed on a royal sheikha.

It didn't matter that, in the concern about his recovery and the future of the monarchy, a candidate for his bride had already been put forward. Though fortunately it had gone no further than that. Isam had agreed only to consider the suggestion, there'd been no announcement. Despite the increasing pressure from senior advisors that he needed to secure the succession soon.

Avril offered a small smile that made his belly tighten. 'It *has* been a lot. I feel like a cushion that's missing half its stuffing.'

'I understand.' He chose his words carefully. He had to take this one slow step at a time rather than spook her. 'Unfortunately, I can't stay in London. There are urgent reasons for me to return to Zahdar. But we need to discuss how we go forward and I don't want to do that long-distance. We need to talk face to face so there are no misunderstandings. Our daughter's future is too important. Do you agree?'

'I do. I've spent a year wallowing in doubt about you, about us.' She stopped, her eyes widening as if surprised at her use of the word *us*. As if she hadn't written off their relationship.

He was startled too, given her earlier deep mistrust.

'So when are you coming back to London?'

'I'm afraid matters at home are such that I won't be able to leave again for quite some time.'

'You're the King. Surely you can make it happen.' She folded her arms. 'If it's important enough to you.'

If only it were that simple.

He could come and go if he wished but there was too much at stake for him to be out of the country for any length of time. Rashid had been emphatic that he could deal with the London situation, as he called it, alone, urging Isam to stay in Zahdar. But Isam had known he had to find out about Avril in person. It was part of finding out about himself.

Meanwhile Hafiz would take advantage of his absence to undermine him further if he could. Who knew what damage Hafiz was doing even now?

'Believe me, Avril, I'm thinking about the long-term needs of Maryam, of you. *Us.*' He let that sink in and saw her eyes widen. 'That's my primary concern but at the same time it's vital I return to Zahdar. So I have a proposition.'

'Go on.'

'Come back with me.' He raised his hand to stop the protest he saw forming on her lips. 'Please hear me before you object.'

Avril gave a small huff of impatience, her mouth forming a pout that should have looked obstinate and annoying. Yet it was so alluring it sparked a flare of heat low in his belly. A flare of hunger.

It was so instantaneous, so absolute, it took Isam a second to find his voice again.

'Come to Zahdar. The pair of you. And your nanny. You can rest and get your strength back after what must have been a tough year. I'll organise comfortable accommodation for you all. While you're there we can take our time making plans for our daughter.'

He saw doubt writ large on her face. 'Think of it as a well-earned holiday.'

Still she hesitated. 'Surely that's risking complications, us coming to your country? Wouldn't it be better to talk here?'

Complications! She and Maryam were already complications that needed to be handled carefully, not just for his sake but for that of the monarchy and potentially the nation.

'I can promise you private accommodation in Zahdar. If you stay here, I fear it won't be long before the press start bothering you. I can't totally protect you from that if you stay.'

'The press!' She looked horrified. 'No one knows about us.'

He lifted tight shoulders and spread his hands. 'Not yet. But since my accident I'm under immense scrutiny. People were concerned for a long time about whether I was fit to rule, given the severity of my injuries.' He refused to use the word enemies. There was no need to scare her.

'Sooner or later someone will take an interest in what I've been doing in London. They'll make a connection to you, and Maryam. Then you'll be hounded every time you step outside your door. Come with me, Avril. I promise to keep you both safe while we plan for the future.'

CHAPTER SEVEN

PRIVATE ACCOMMODATION, HE'D SAID.

A place to relax and recuperate after a difficult year, he'd said. A place where they could take their time to discuss the future.

Well, two out of three wasn't bad, she supposed.

Avril had seen Isam daily since arriving in Zahdar four days ago. He seemed fascinated by Maryam, wanting to spend time with her and Avril when his schedule permitted, but so far there hadn't been enough time for them to discuss the future in any detail.

Do you really want to?

There would be difficult decisions to make, compromises she wasn't looking forward to, because she couldn't deny Isam the right to know his daughter. Inevitably that would mean time when Maryam would be with her father, not her.

Avril had no illusions. Isam was a king, he wouldn't spend his precious time with his daughter at Avril's tiny London house.

Yet she couldn't imagine being parted from her little girl. The thought made Avril's chest tighten and her hands tremble.

A gusty sigh escaped as she folded her arms, her mind shying from that horrible thought to her surroundings.

The accommodation Isam had organised was private as he'd promised and quiet enough to relax in, if you could forget it was in the heart of Zahdar's royal palace!

It was a small mercy, she supposed, that this luxurious suite of rooms didn't have ceilings gilded with real gold like some of the rooms they'd passed on the way here. Nor were there columns studded with rubies and lapis lazuli like in the entrance colonnade where they'd entered the enormous complex. And that, she'd learned later, hadn't even been the main entrance!

Yet everything here, from the artworks to the vast proportions and sumptuous furnishings, screamed *royal*. Her en-suite bathroom could accommodate a hockey team, the sunken bath clearly designed for more than one person.

An illicit image crept into Avril's mind, of sharing it with Isam. Even after a year she had perfect recall of his lean, powerful body and how it had felt, naked, against hers.

She shivered, not with cold but with a heated awareness that belied the fact she'd given birth only four months ago.

Surely new mothers weren't supposed to be interested in sexy men. Particularly men who'd lost interest in *them* as objects of desire.

Isam was the perfect host. But he never, by so much as a sidelong glance, gave any indication he viewed her as an attractive woman any more. As if the carnal heat saturating his gaze on their one night together had been a mirage.

What do you expect? The man's forgotten that night, erased it from his memory.

If it had been significant enough to him he'd remember. You weren't significant enough.

The carping inner voice had only made a reappearance in Avril's life since Isam left her without a word in London. Before that, with Cilla's help, she'd virtually banished the old self-doubt from her life, the belief she wasn't special enough to make her parents stay. Wasn't special enough to inspire love.

Avril stiffened. She was an adult and knew she wasn't responsible for her parents' actions.

She was capable and strong. Yet she felt undone by the insistent tug of attraction for Isam that still lurked deep inside. Even though to him she was merely an inconvenient problem. She was a complete stranger to the one man to whom she'd ever given her trust. How that hurt.

She grimaced. Scratch the surface and there, after all, was the needy little girl she'd once been. The one who'd cried when Mummy left and didn't come back. Who'd stifled tears when Daddy went away too. But at least by then she'd had Cilla and some stability in her world.

Which is what Maryam will need. Stability and love, lots of it.

She'd deliver that for her daughter. She'd do everything necessary to ensure it. Including negotiating a shared parenting arrangement with a royal sheikh!

Avril stared out at their private courtyard.

Filled with scented flowers, it was glorious, so pleasing to the senses that even she could tell every plant, every path and fountain had been put together by a master. As for the pool with its hand-painted tiles and cushioned sunbeds with embroidered silk canopies and gauzy curtains...

The whole place was beyond anything she could have dreamt. Was it any wonder she felt out of place?

Cilla had raised her to be independent and practical, and Avril had worked for some powerful people, occasionally glimpsing their more rarefied worlds.

But this was on a different scale. This wasn't just wealth. This was royal privilege, complete with liveried staff, a

palace bigger than her old neighbourhood, and a labyrin-
thine web of protocols governing everything right down to
modes of address and appropriate clothing. She knew from
the compendium of information that had been supplied to
help her and Bethany acclimatise.

Acclimatise! Avril had read it from cover to cover and
wished Isam had found them rooms in an anonymous hotel
in the city.

Here everything reminded her of the immense power
Isam wielded. The imbalance between them.

What was she, an ordinary woman from an ordinary
background, doing here? Already she felt at a disadvantage
and they hadn't even begun their negotiations.

'Avril?'

Isam's rich baritone slid across her skin as if conjured
by her thoughts. Her flesh prickled, every fine hair on her
body standing alert while her heartbeat quickened.

She whipped around to discover Isam in the doorway.
Instead of a dark suit, he wore long white robes and a head-
scarf secured with a twist of dark cord. The simple clothes
suited him, emphasising his height and the lean strength
of his body.

A dull throb started low in her abdomen and she fought
to ignore it. She no longer had the defence of anger against
him. The news he hadn't deliberately cut her out of his life
changed everything.

Avril feared that at the core of her jumbled emotions was
something too strong, too dangerous to her peace of mind.

'I knocked, several times.'

She nodded, throat catching on a stifled breath of min-
gled appreciation and nerves. 'Please, come in.'

Even though she wanted to tell him to leave. She didn't
feel up to the discussion they had to have. She knew, no mat-

ter how reasonable he was, that she'd hate the outcome. The idea of leaving her precious girl for even a short length of time, a couple of days, even weeks, churned nausea through her belly.

He glanced around the large room. 'Maryam's sleeping?'

That twist of sensation low in her body changed to something like disappointment.

What sort of woman is jealous of her own daughter?

You should be pleased he's so interested in Maryam. That's as it should be, a father wanting to see his girl.

This isn't about you.

Avril stood straighter. 'Yes, she's sleeping. Bethany is with her, while I—'

Isam crossed the room. It was less than twenty-four hours since she'd seen him, yet she was struck anew by the depth of her response. The softening, low in her body. The spark of heat. The humming need.

As if her body had awoken to one man and one alone. A terrifying thought!

'You…?'

She'd been going to venture out of the palace for an hour, take up the standing offer of a guide to take her into the city. She'd spent too long here, stewing over things she couldn't change, growing more rather than less nervous by the day despite the extra rest she was getting.

'It doesn't matter. Won't you sit down? I want to talk to you about Maryam.'

'She's all right? There's nothing wrong?' Concern sharpened his voice.

'She's fine. As I said, she's sleeping.'

Avril perched on the edge of a damask-covered settee and watched him take a seat opposite.

'Excellent. But if ever you have concerns, at any hour of the day or night, we can summon the palace doctor.'

She frowned, imagining an echo of anxiety in his tone.

She must be mistaken. Maryam had shown no negative effects from the travel. As for Isam anxious… He was one of the most competent, confident men she knew. Surely as Sheikh he had the power to make problems vanish from his life.

Avril wished she could do the same.

Lacing her fingers, she drew a deep breath. She couldn't put this off any longer. 'It's time we talked about Maryam.'

Isam inclined his head. 'Yes, and I want to know more about us.'

'Us?' That hit out of the blue. 'There isn't an us.'

Was it imagination or did the proud angles of his face grow more pronounced, more severe? 'Yet here we are, parents with a child. I want to know more about our relationship. How we came together.'

Avril had assumed that after pregnancy and giving birth, with strangers performing intimate examinations and procedures on her body, nothing could make her blush.

She was wrong. Heat surged up her throat and into her cheeks. She was tempted to blurt *in the usual way*, but stopped herself in time.

He's not asking what the sex was like.

'Does it matter now? The important thing is our daughter.'

He leaned closer, elbows on the arms of his chair and fingers touching. 'As you say, she's paramount. But… I feel at a disadvantage. You have full recall of something intimate and significant between us and I have none.' His mouth tightened and she saw something in his eyes that looked like vulnerability. 'It's a terrible thing to have blank spaces in your memory with no understanding of how you behaved.'

The heat intensified in Avril's cheeks. Not from embarrassment but from shame that she hadn't thought about this from Isam's perspective. The reality of memory loss was something she could barely conceive. He shouldn't have to beg to find out more.

'Of course. I'm sorry.' She cleared her throat. 'We worked together for several months before you came to London. Our working relationship was good. You trusted me and I handled the work well.'

'I didn't interview you in person?'

'You did, but via a video call, after all I was going to be your *virtual* PA, working remotely. You also set me some tasks to do then assessed my performance.' Still he didn't look convinced. 'My previous employer, Berthold Keller, recommended me to you. I'd worked for him for several years but he knew I wanted to work from home.'

Isam nodded. 'Why did you want to work from home?'

Avril paused, fighting a natural instinct for privacy. But there was no harm in sharing this. Besides, guilt at being so thoughtless about his amnesia spurred her on. 'I lived with my great-aunt. She was well in spirit and mind but growing physically frail. I wanted to be on hand to help her.'

'She shares your house? I didn't see her in London.'

Avril looked down at her hands, clenched in her lap. 'Actually, I lived in *her* house. She raised me. But she died after I began working for you.'

'I'm sorry for your loss, Avril. Was it after my time in London?'

She looked up to see dark pewter eyes fixed on her, full of sympathy. She drew a wobbly breath. 'No, just before.'

He jerked back in his seat. 'You were bereaved when we met in person? Did I know?'

'You had no idea.' It wasn't something she'd wanted to speak about. 'It was actually a relief to spend that week with you, concentrating on work rather than everything else.'

The funeral and its aftermath had left her drained. Did that explain her fixation with Isam? Her no-holds-barred need for him? Maybe her yearning had been some sort of reaction to grief.

So what's your excuse now? Cilla's been gone for more than a year and he only has to look at you to make you melt.

Avril lifted her head and discovered his expression was sombre. 'I owe you an apology, Avril.'

She frowned. His amnesia explained why he hadn't been in contact. 'What for?'

'For seducing you when you were my employee. For crossing a boundary that should never have been crossed. For taking advantage of you in your grief.' He shook his head, his gaze leaving hers to fix on a point behind her. 'For taking your innocence. My behaviour was—'

'You've got it wrong!' She leaned forward, aghast at his misunderstanding. 'You didn't seduce me. We… It was utterly mutual.'

'Nevertheless, given our professional relationship—'

'You're not hearing me. We were both…attracted.' What an anaemic word for that full-blooded, desperate craving. Avril didn't have words to describe the urgent compulsion she'd felt that night. 'We'd both been fighting it, and you were adamant we shouldn't act on it, precisely because I worked for you. But I insisted. I wanted, needed you that night as I'd never needed anyone before.'

It was simultaneously terrifying and liberating to admit it. But seeing Isam's anxiety over what he believed his unpardonable actions, she was determined to clear any mis-understanding. The man had suffered enough, losing his father and his memory, without adding to his misery.

It was a relief to know her original assessment of him was right. She'd spent most of the last year despising him for his apparent decision to cut her from his life. This proof of his true character reassured and warmed her.

Not for her own sake, since there'd be no going back to their fleeting relationship. But it was a relief to know Maryam's father was a decent man.

'You didn't pressure me, Isam. On the contrary, you said no, but I wouldn't listen. I understood your scruples. I knew it could be no more than a single night. But I—'

Had to have you.

'I initiated it. I coaxed you into it.'

'You're saying *you* seduced *me*?'

Heat tinged her cheeks and ears. That made her sound like some femme fatale, alluring and confident. In fact she'd simply been desperate. She shrugged. 'Yes.'

Those grey eyes were narrowed on her. What did he see? A weary mother with bags under her eyes. Hardly a temptress.

She shifted in her seat, uncomfortable, not with what she'd done that night, but knowing he was wondering why he'd slept with someone so ordinary. She'd seen the old media reports, the photos of him at high-profile events with glamorous, sophisticated women.

Avril sat straighter, needing to change the subject. 'That doesn't matter now. It's in the past. We need to discuss Maryam's future.'

His stare told her he knew she was changing the subject deliberately. But to her relief, instead of objecting, he nodded. 'That's why I carved out time from today's schedule.

We need to make some decisions. Nothing matters more than our daughter.'

On that they both agreed. Maybe this might be easier than she'd anticipated. Easier yet still distressing.

'She can't inherit the throne, can she? It's males only?'

'As the constitution stands, yes.'

That was a relief. Not that she wanted her daughter to miss out on opportunities, far from it. But if she'd been heir to a throne, Avril might have had a fight on her hands, raising their daughter in the UK.

'Why do you ask? What do you want for Maryam?'

'Don't worry, Isam. I don't have royal aspirations for her. I just want her to have a loving, secure home life. To have a decent education and a chance to pursue her dreams when she's older.'

'Good. I want something very similar for her.'

Similar but not the same? Avril moistened her lips, about to ask where they differed but he was already speaking.

'There are excellent schools and universities in Zahdar.'

She stiffened. 'And in the UK.'

'I know. I attended one for several years. My grandmother was English and a few years being educated in another country was very beneficial.'

The flutter of anxiety in Avril's stomach eased. So he was talking about Maryam, when older, spending some time here. Avril couldn't object to that. Even in the months when she'd thought Isam had cruelly deserted her, she'd been determined her daughter would learn something of her father's culture and heritage. Growing up with two languages and two cultures could only be an asset.

'That sounds reasonable.'

His lips quirked up at the corners in the hint of a smile that brought back memories of that week in London. Memories of his warmth and ready charm, how enthralled she'd been.

But it wasn't all memory. Little shivers of awareness were even now thrumming through her core. Her nipples had peaked at the mere hint of his smile.

Avril crossed her arms then uncrossed them, shifting in her seat. 'But that's years away. In the meantime we need to think about access.' She paused, wishing she didn't have to say it. 'I'm assuming you want to be involved?'

Something flared in those grey eyes. Something that saturated her body with heat then left it shivering with cold. Did she imagine his mouth tightened?

'You assume right. I'm her father. I'll be very much involved.'

He didn't raise his voice but it had a sharp edge that made her think of honed steel.

Avril made herself nod and smile. 'Just checking. I didn't know, given your royal responsibilities—'

'I take those very seriously, Avril. But nothing is more important to me than Maryam's well-being. Than family.'

Emotion coursed through her. If things had been different, if they'd shared more than a one-night stand, his words would have been music to her ears. She'd imagined that one day she'd find love with a steadfast, wonderful man and together they'd create a loving family. In other circumstances, Isam would have made a perfect father and partner.

Meanwhile, her little girl deserved a caring family. Parents who'd always be there for her. Not deserting her and making her feel she didn't deserve their attention.

It was only now she had a daughter that Avril felt the full weight of anger at the way her own parents had treated her. For years she'd felt bereft and insecure, her self-confidence damaged until Cilla did her best to change that. Now she was determined that her daughter wouldn't be abandoned as she'd been.

'I want to be part of Maryam's world. I want to be with her as she grows up, someone she can depend on for love, guidance and support.'

She felt her eyes grow round. That sounded more hands-on than she'd expected. 'And I assume you want the same, don't you, Avril?'

'Of course. But I'm certainly not going to hand her over to be raised elsewhere.'

Isam nodded. 'I agree. We both want her to have the best and we both need to be involved. So there's one obvious solution. We marry and raise her together.'

His mouth curved into a smile that didn't reach his eyes. They looked sombre and she felt a chill run along her back-bone, because she knew he was serious.

Yet the idea was preposterous. 'Marry? We can't marry. You're a king and I'm your PA. *Was* your PA.' His mind-ers at that meeting in London had made it clear her ser-vices wouldn't be required any longer. 'Royals don't marry women they barely know. Commoners from another coun-try.'

His smile became a twist of the lips. 'You'd be surprised at how often royals marry virtual strangers, for the good of their country. And there's nothing preventing a king from marrying outside his own nation.'

'But I'm…' Ordinary. Unremarkable. Not glamorous or well connected. 'Not cut out to be a queen.'

'You love your daughter, don't you? We'd be marrying for her. As for the rest, you can learn our customs, learn to be royal. If I hired you as my PA, you must be clever and diligent, trustworthy and dedicated.' He leaned forward, his voice coaxing. 'I don't pretend it will always be easy. But

I'll be by your side, *on* your side, yours and Maryam's. You can rely on me. I'll help you through the challenges and it will be worth it to give our daughter a stable, loving home.'

Avril opened her mouth, about to list all the logical, sensible reasons why it was a far-fetched idea.

But his words echoed in her head.

'You can rely on me. A stable, loving home.'

The sort of home her parents hadn't provided, because she hadn't been their priority. Her mother had deserted her to take up with a new lover and the freedom of life on the road. Her father, who'd always travelled for work, had gone for longer and longer periods rather than less while Avril grew up. Until finally he fell in love with a Canadian woman and followed her across the Atlantic to start a new family.

And here was Isam, offering marriage, willing to withstand the inevitable backlash if he married a foreigner with nothing to recommend her as Queen, all for the sake of Maryam.

That he was a man who felt strongly, not just about duty, but about their daughter, was obvious. When he married he expected it to be permanent. It was there in his grave expression and the stillness of his tall frame.

Avril's heart squeezed. That he would do this for their daughter.

But what about you? What about your happiness? Are you willing to throw that away?

But would it be throwing it away? Surely it would be building a future for Maryam. And who was to say Avril wouldn't find happiness here with Isam and her daughter?

It struck her that while she'd inherited her mother's colouring and her father's organisational skills, she was fundamentally different to them. She might not be the world's most adept mother. She still had a lot to learn. But when it came to priorities she put her daughter's needs first.

Avril sighed and sank back in her seat. 'What if you fall in love? Would you want a divorce?'

He was already shaking his head by the time she stopped speaking. 'I've never been romantically inclined. I've known many women and never imagined myself in love. I was raised to expect an arranged marriage.' He paused, pinioning her gaze so it felt as if he saw deep into her soul. 'I'm proposing a *real* marriage, Avril. We'd be partners and lovers. And you have my word that I'll be faithful.'

She blinked in astonishment as unmistakable heat fizzed in her veins, coalescing low in her core. Sexual anticipation. She recognised it now and it made a liar of her attempts to tell herself this was totally about Maryam. For there was part of her that wanted Isam, just as she had from the first.

But suggesting marriage was one thing. Vowing fidelity was another. 'You don't even know if we're compatible—'

'I may not remember the details, Avril. But the fact I broke every rule so I could have you tells its own story.' Those serious eyes glazed hot, intensifying the eager, melting sensation deep inside. As if he now remembered that night and the pinnacles of ecstasy they'd reached together. 'We're sexually compatible. Everything tells me I trusted you and I see no reason for that to change. I hope you trust me too. Plus we have Maryam.' He lifted those wide shoulders in a shrug. 'We have a better basis for marriage than many.'

He made it sound so reasonable. Instead of utterly shocking.

'Once I give my vow, I won't break it. I'm a man of my word.'

She believed him. The gravity of his expression and the tone of his voice, plus all she knew about him, said so.

'I take my promises seriously too.'

If she were to agree to this, she'd commit wholeheart-edly.

'Excellent. So you—?'

'It's an...extraordinary idea. I'll need time to think about it.'

His expression told her it wasn't what he wanted to hear. Impatience danced in his glittering eyes. But instead of trying to push her into a decision, he nodded.

'Naturally. But time's of the essence. The palace staff are discreet but the longer you're here, the greater the risk the news will leak. I want to control the release of information, rather than have rumours circulate. I won't allow anyone to turn you and our daughter into fodder for gossip.'

It was a reminder that she'd stepped into a new world under the public spotlight.

Not what she wanted.

He looked at his watch then rose. 'I'll expect your answer by the end of the week.'

CHAPTER EIGHT

SHE WAS DUE to give Isam an answer on the biggest decision of her life.

Was it any wonder Avril couldn't settle?

She'd slept a lot and swum in the clear waters of the courtyard's private pool. She'd begun to feel refreshed in a way she hadn't for ages. Yet she was on edge, and of course Maryam picked up on her agitation, growing more fidgety.

Bethany had practically pushed Avril out the door today, suggesting she go outside while she settled the baby. Avril had thought about exploring the city but decided against it. What she needed was to stretch her legs in solitude, not listening to the patter of a guide.

So she left their secluded part of the palace for the grand gardens within the palace compound. She wanted space. Walking always helped her sort out her thoughts.

A staff member ushered her through magnificent doors onto a broad, marble-lined portico. Avril's breath caught at the beauty of the gardens before her, sloping down past a channel of water and fountains, into rambling parkland.

Someone had spent a lot of time and effort ensuring there was plentiful water for this beautiful green space.

Movement further along the pillared terrace drew her attention. She turned to see a group of people gathered there in the shade, heads turning her way. Hurriedly she plonked on her wide-brimmed hat and strode away.

She didn't want to draw attention to herself. She didn't know what the press was like in Zahdar, but at home the unmarried mother of a king's child would be fodder for screaming headlines and gossip.

Would it be any different if you married him? There'd still be gossip and headlines because you're so unsuited to be Queen. The whole idea is preposterous.

But if they didn't marry, what was the alternative? Sharing Maryam, six months here and six in London? What was to stop the paparazzi making their lives hell in the UK?

Isam would give Maryam the stability and care Avril craved for her. And there'd be no tug-of-love separations as their daughter passed between London and Zahdar.

But it would mean putting yourself in the power of a man you barely know.

Except, she decided as she strode beyond the fountains and into the shrubbery, she felt she *did* know Isam. A man of his word. Strong, yes, but caring.

Even since coming to his palace Avril had seen enough to know he loved Maryam. There was a tenderness, an excitement and pride when he was with their baby, that made Avril's heart squeeze and her insides turn to mush. And not merely because there was something intrinsically attractive about a big, powerful man gently cradling a tiny bub.

She walked for an hour, weighing her options. Yet still she wasn't ready to make a decision. But it was getting hot and Maryam would be awake.

Avril followed the long mirror pools up the rise towards the palace. She'd almost reached it when voices caught her attention. She saw that group again, still clustered in the now scant shade.

She noticed a walking frame and a wheelchair and heads of grey and white hair.

Avril frowned. She'd grown up surrounded by Cilla's elderly friends. She respected and liked them. She also understood the frailties of age. Surely these old ladies shouldn't be out here as the heat intensified?

Caution warred with concern for about a second before she headed towards them.

They were dressed beautifully, as if for a special occasion. Many fanned themselves and several drooped. She couldn't see so much as a cup or glass between them.

She paused, searching her scant knowledge of Arabic. 'Hello. Are you thirsty? Would you like a drink?'

A chorus of greetings came her way, along with smiles and curious looks. One, tall and upright, nodded and spoke at some length.

'I'm sorry. I only know a few words. Do you speak English?'

Murmurs greeted that, but the woman nodded. 'I do. Thank you for your offer. Drinks would be very welcome.' She tilted her head enquiringly. 'Your Arabic may be limited but it's very good. Do you work in the palace?'

The palace employees were perfectly groomed and attired, whereas Avril suspected her cotton dress was crumpled and less than pristine after unsuccessfully trying to settle Maryam. 'No, I'm a visitor.'

Curiosity was bright in the other woman's eyes. 'We're visitors too. We had an appointment to see His Majesty. But there's been some delay.'

And they'd been left out *here*? Something wasn't right. Quite apart from the unsuitability of leaving them in the heat, the palace was full of comfortable rooms.

Avril covered her concern with a smile and inclined her head. 'I'll be back shortly.'

She hurried to the double doors, the temperature dropping deliciously as she stepped inside. The man who'd shown her into the garden was hurrying away. He didn't pause when she called him, as if not hearing.

She hesitated, knowing she couldn't leave the women in the heat any longer. They needed drinks but they needed to be in the cool too. But where?

More footsteps sounded, coming down a long corridor from the opposite direction.

Avril rushed to intercept a man carrying a bulging file. He looked slightly familiar, as if she'd seen him in the distance during her tour of the palace. 'Excuse me.'

'Yes, madam?'

'Can you help me? I need a room, large enough to seat a group of about fifteen guests in comfort. Not on hard seats but in comfortable chairs. Is there something like that in this part of the palace?'

'Well, I'm sure if you put in a request—'

'I'm afraid there's no time for a request. The room is needed *now*.'

Avril read his surprise and feared that if she didn't press her case he might leave, like the servant who'd pretended not to hear. One of the old ladies hadn't looked well and Avril worried. She stood straighter, lifting her chin and sweeping off her sunhat.

'There's been an unfortunate mix-up. The Sheikh has guests who have been left waiting outside in the heat for more than an hour. *Elderly* guests. It's not appropriate. We need a room for them, the more comfortable, the better. We need drinks immediately. A couple of them look particularly fatigued and I'm worried about dehydration.'

The man opened his mouth to speak but Avril pressed on. 'And food too, please. We also need to inform His Majesty so he can see them as soon as possible. Can you do that?'

To her relief, instead of arguing, he gave a small bow. 'You can rely on me. This way.'

He led her down the corridor, opening a door onto a spacious, opulent sitting room. The couches looked comfortable and there were small tables that would be perfect for drinks.

'Will it do?' He nodded to doors on the far side of the room. 'Bathroom facilities through there.'

Avril grinned, relieved. 'Thank you, it's perfect.'

His rather stern features transformed as he smiled. 'Excellent. You bring the guests and I'll see to the rest. When I speak to the Sheikh, who shall I say arranged this?'

She hesitated, feeling she shouldn't broadcast her name to a stranger since she didn't want to stir gossip. But it was too late. 'Ms Rodgers. Thank you so much, Mr—'

But he was already hurrying away, pulling out his phone.

Ten minutes later the women were all comfortably seated. Scant moments after that a parade of staff brought trays of cold drinks, delicate fruit ices and platters of finger food. They circulated among the women, offering refreshment and delicately embroidered napkins.

Soon after, hot drinks arrived including mint tea, cinnamon tea and coffee. Platters of hot food arrived after that, all provided by smiling, attentive maids.

Avril straightened from moving a small table closer to one of the guests, and looked around, satisfied.

'Very nicely done, my dear.' It was the tall woman who'd since introduced herself as Hana Bishara. 'I couldn't have done better myself.'

This was obviously high praise. 'Thank you. Though the kitchen staff have done all the work.'

The food looked and smelled delicious, reminding her she'd skimped on breakfast and she was starving. As soon as Isam arrived, or someone from his office, she'd leave to get her own lunch. Her breasts felt tight too, a reminder that Maryam would need feeding soon.

'You obviously have a talent for organisation, and the authority to make things happen here.'

Again Avril recognised curiosity in Hana's expression.

'Not authority. I just pointed out to the staff that there'd been some mistake, and requested refreshments.'

'If you say so. Ah, here's His Majesty.'

There was a ripple of movement as all the guests rose then bent their heads before the Sheikh, who paused in the doorway, flanked by a number of serious-faced staff.

Over their heads, Isam's eyes met Avril's and heat skimmed her flesh. In that second it felt as though something powerful passed between them. Understanding. Recognition. And something far more powerful.

Or maybe you're imagining it because you want to believe he didn't just propose out of duty. Because you're tempted to accept.

But Avril wasn't into self-deception. His proposal was pragmatic, nothing more.

Yet as he crossed the room towards them, she couldn't prevent the flutter of excitement in her chest. Those grey eyes seemed to flare as they met hers.

Maybe it was time for an eye test.

'Your Majesty.' Her quick curtsey felt ungainly. 'May I present Ms Hana Bishara.'

He greeted the older woman in Arabic then continued in English. 'My sincere apologies for the discomfort your group has suffered. My staff tell me there was a problem with the timetable. But that's no excuse. I'm deeply interested in your delegation's views.'

'Your Majesty is very kind.'

'Not at all. Perhaps you'd like to introduce me to the members of your group.'

As he turned towards her companions, Isam murmured to Avril, 'Thank you for saving the day. We'll speak later.'

His words and his smile warmed her to the core.

Was she really so needy, basking in his approval for something any sensible person would have done? Yet she found herself smiling as she exchanged farewells with the women.

It was late when Isam finally left his office. His already full schedule had been disrupted by the lunchtime fiasco, throwing the rest of his timetable out completely.

It had been a near disaster. If not for Avril…

His jaw clenched so hard pain circled the base of his skull. It wasn't the first inexplicable problem. There'd been a series of difficult, potentially embarrassing situations. The common factor was that in every case the mistake led back to *his* office.

The women's delegation today, there to advocate for better support for the elderly, had been told he'd specifically requested they attend today, whereas his official appointment diary showed them coming tomorrow.

He knocked on the door to Avril's suite, and hearing nothing, knocked again.

A muffled voice called from inside. Opening the door, he heard Avril, in another room. 'I'll be out in a minute. Maryam and I are just finishing up.'

His daughter was still awake? Isam's spirits lightened.

She was the perfect antidote to the pressures and problems weighing down on him.

He closed the door and crossed the sitting room, only to halt in an open doorway at the sight before him.

He'd imagined Avril was changing a nappy. Instead he found her seated in a comfortable chair, her long hair curtaining her shoulders, head bent as she smiled down at the baby who'd clearly just finished feeding. Avril's blouse was open, one perfect breast bared.

The air caught in his lungs.

She looked the archetypal mother, tender and life-giving.

And sexy. So sexy Isam felt his blood rush to his groin. Carnal hunger ripped through him, weighting his muscles and tightening his lungs. Hunger and something else that felt like possessiveness.

Given the fact each day brought more teasing memories of them making love, it shouldn't surprise him. He remembered her exquisite softness, her delightful eagerness, her expression as he tipped her over the edge into bliss. She'd looked at him in wonder, as if he weren't a mere man but some hero. As if he'd made the world stop for her alone.

Those memories, though fragmented, made him wish—

'Isam! I thought you were Bethany.'

As she spoke she pulled her blouse closed, a delicate rose pink tinting her cheeks. She looked adorable. Though the word didn't do her justice. It was too passive for such a vibrant woman.

'I said we'd talk. I'm afraid this was the earliest I could get away.'

He walked forward, arms out. 'Let me take her while you do up your buttons.'

Though it was a shame for Avril to cover up.

She nodded and he gently took their baby. *Their baby.*

The wonder of it never ceased to amaze him. But his joy was undercut by the way Avril flinched at his inadvertent touch. So different from when they'd made love.

Isam was eager to renew that intimacy. But he couldn't push. It was more important, for now, to convince her to marry him.

He gathered up little Maryam, smiling down into her long-lashed eyes, and turned away, giving Avril privacy. The little one waved a hand in the air and when he touched it, a tiny fist wrapped around his index finger.

Everything in Isam melted. All the barriers he'd built around himself in the last year. Essential barriers that had allowed him to deal with grief for his father and the loss of his own autonomy.

That was how it felt, as if he'd lost himself, or an essential part, along with his memory.

But feeling his daughter's surprisingly powerful grip, experiencing his own rush of love, made his shattered self seem whole.

As did his longing for Avril. For the first time in a year, he wanted a woman. Not just wanted. Craved. It was a physical hunger yet a superstitious part of him almost believed she could make him complete again. Since meeting her, memories had started trickling into his brain.

'What are you singing?'

He turned to find her close, all buttoned up. 'Just a lullaby. I used to sing it for my sister.'

'You cared for her?'

Of course he'd cared for her. Then he realised what Avril meant. 'My mother died, having her. I was eleven and my father explained that while a nanny would look after her, it was important Nur knew from the beginning that she was loved and part of the family.'

He stopped, hearing his voice turned to gravel. His sister had died years ago yet still, sometimes, the grief hit as if fresh.

Warmth circled his upper arm as Avril touched his sleeve. 'I'm sorry you lost your sister. I can't imagine what that would be like.'

When he nodded but didn't say anything she continued. 'I grew up as an only child. Though I've got half-siblings now.' Her tone was flat.

'You don't get on with them?'

Avril's mouth crimped into a crooked line. 'I've never met them. When I was in my early teens my father migrated to marry a Canadian. I've never met his wife or their children.'

Fury scythed through him, and outrage on her behalf. 'He didn't invite you to go with him? He left you with your great-aunt?'

She shrugged but her shoulders looked tight. 'He wasn't around much by then anyway. He travelled a lot for work.'

In his arms the baby squirmed and he realised he held her too tight. He eased his grip, rocking her gently. 'You didn't want to go with him?'

What sort of man abandoned his daughter?

Avril lifted Maryam, now yawning, from his arms and put her in the cot. 'By that stage we weren't close.'

Isam bit down a scathing observation about her father. It might relieve his feelings but at what cost to hers? 'And your mother?'

The brief report he'd received had been focused on Avril's professional life, not her family history.

'She died a long time ago.' She cut him off before he could express sympathy. 'It's okay. I was so little I barely remember her. She left to be with someone else and then died in an accident a few years later.'

Isam had come here focused on the difficulties of his day. Talking to Avril put those in perspective.

He wanted to gather her to him and ease her pain, an instinctive response that by its very nature made him pause. That, and her expression, which almost dared him to feel sorry for her.

'No wonder you're such an independent, capable person,' he said as he gestured for her to precede him into the sitting room.

When they were both seated she responded. 'I'm glad you think so.'

'I *know* so. The last few days I've been getting snippets of memory back.' He saw her sit up, alert. 'When I was in London that week, we had meetings in the conference room of my suite.'

She nodded, her voice eager. 'You remember our time together?'

In truth what he remembered most clearly were the physical sensations and erotic highs of sexual intimacy. Recalling the tight embrace of her body turned him hard with wanting. Memories of caresses and whispered endearments were a siren song that grew in intensity each day.

Better to focus on what they'd done out of bed.

'I remember some of it. A couple of interviews. A man named Drucker, wasn't it?'

Avril sat forward, hands clasped together. 'That's right.'

'You didn't approve of him.' Isam smiled. 'I recall you were quite fluent about his flaws.'

She lifted her shoulders, this time the movement seemed easier. 'You asked for my opinion.'

'Which proves I trusted you.'

Isam was more than capable of making up his own mind, so the fact he'd asked for her input was telling.

'Is that all you remember?'

'Bits and pieces.' He still didn't recall how they'd ended up in bed together, just the delight when they did. Despite Avril's assurances, he was still uncomfortable, wondering if she'd downplayed his actions and he *had* taken advantage. 'But enough for today to make sense.'

'Today? What do you mean?'

'You remedied a potentially disastrous situation with speed and aplomb. I'm grateful for your intervention.'

The colour in her cheeks deepened and her eyes shone. Avril liked being appreciated. Who didn't? But she looked as if he'd handed her a prize, complimenting her on her competence.

Isam thought of what she'd revealed about her family. Having been abandoned by those who should have loved her, did she find validation in achievement?

'Anyone would have done the same.'

He shook his head. 'Not nearly so well. You made the ladies feel valued and appreciated. You anticipated their needs with genuine consideration. They were full of praise for you. I hear you even exchanged pleasantries in my language. When did you have time to learn that?'

'I only know basic phrases. I tried to learn a little for Maryam. I wanted her to grow up knowing something of your culture and language.'

Isam was stunned. 'Even though you thought I'd dumped you?'

Those warm, brown eyes looked away, over his shoulder. 'Especially because of that. I thought if she couldn't rely on her father, it would be up to me to help teach her.'

And she'd called their daughter a name that would work

both in England and in Zahdar. For a moment he was silent, awed by her generosity, her determination to make their child's life as rich and meaningful as she could.

'I'll help you learn. You can have a tutor, but I'll help you myself too.'

'While I'm here.'

He stiffened. Was she signalling she wanted to leave? He'd brought her here to marry her. That hadn't changed.

Initially he'd been busy sorting through the difficulties of taking her as his bride so he could counter them. All the ways she wouldn't fit in.

But there were positives. She was kind-hearted but sensible. She was good with people, *his* people. Today she'd held her own with as much assurance as any royal and in trying circumstances, thinking quickly and clearly. No wonder he'd hired her as his PA. She was determined to do her best for their child and he believed, once they were wed, she'd be loyal and supportive.

As for their sex life…he couldn't imagine anyone more compatible.

He *wanted* Avril. She had the values and traits he desired in a partner.

And you've never felt so enthusiastic about the idea of marrying any other woman.

'About that,' he said. 'I'm here for your answer. It's the end of the week and I'd like to announce our engagement sooner rather than later. If you agree.' He paused, watching her tense. Many women would leap at the chance to be his queen, but not Avril. 'After today rumours will be flying about my uncommon guest.'

'It's one thing to make a baby. It's quite another to become a royal—'

'I know it's daunting, but you can do it. Most of being

royal is about working hard and putting the needs of other people first. You demonstrated that today and you did it without fuss or panic. You were a natural.'

Yet she looked unconvinced. 'I'm used to being the gofer, the assistant, not the one in charge.'

Isam's laughter escaped. 'Oh, I think you'll do very well. You had no hesitation ordering one of the most senior men in the kingdom to do your bidding.'

Her eyes rounded. 'Sorry? You mean the man who organised the food?'

Isam's smile widened. 'I do. He's head of one of the foremost families in the country and a senior government minister.'

For the first time Avril seemed lost for words.

'He was most impressed with your take-charge attitude in a crisis. In fact he asked if you might be interested in joining our diplomatic team.'

To his delight, she chuckled, reminding him of times he'd now recalled when they'd shared a joke while working together. 'I'm glad he didn't take offence. After that other man turned away when I called him for help, I wasn't sure if he'd listen.'

'Other man? What did he look like?'

'About my height, slim, with a beard. He was hanging around near the doors when I went outside and when I came back. I was sure he'd heard me call but he hurried away.'

Isam filed the information away for later. For now he had a more important issue to deal with.

'You'll make an excellent queen. And I'll be there at your side.'

Her gaze caught his and a frisson of heat rippled through him. 'But I don't know the country or customs—'

'Nor did my grandmother when she came from England.

But she was happy here and much loved by the nation as well as the family.' He paused, considering what arguments might sway Avril. 'Here you'll have purpose and a rewarding life, quite apart from the wealth I can offer. We can build a family, a secure world for our little girl. A place where she and you belong. A loving home. Isn't that what you want for her?'

She licked her lips but didn't answer and Isam, an expert at commercial and diplomatic negotiations, felt his stomach churn with nerves.

'What do you say, Avril?'

His heart hammered as she took her time responding. Tension drew his skin tight. She couldn't refuse him!

Finally, she nodded but she didn't smile. 'Very well. I'll marry you, Isam.'

CHAPTER NINE

RELIEF COURSED THROUGH Isam's veins, making him light-headed for a second.

Her agreement secured Maryam's future.

But this wasn't just about his daughter. He wanted Avril with a visceral need he couldn't explain. Not just as the mother of his child. But not just as a sexual partner either, despite the throb low in his body.

What then? This wasn't a romance.

He shied from the thought. He had no time for sentiment, he had a nation to secure. Besides, all the people he'd ever loved had been taken from him. He wasn't interested in opening his heart up to anyone and risking more grief.

Except for Maryam. How could he not love the tiny mite who was his own flesh and blood?

'Excellent.' He kept his tone measured, disguising a disturbing jostle of emotions. 'Together we can build a solid marriage and a wonderful future for our daughter.'

'I…hope so.'

Hardly an effusive agreement. Isam battled annoyance at her lack of excitement.

He knew Avril wanted the best for their baby, but surely he hadn't been mistaken, believing he read attraction in her unguarded looks.

No, he *couldn't* have been mistaken. She wanted him, and he'd been her first, her only lover. That gave him an advantage he could use.

But not now. She needed time.

He'd be taking another long, cold shower tonight.

The gravity of her expression quenched any feeling of celebration. She looked more doubtful than convinced, as if unsure she'd done the right thing.

And she doesn't know the half of the problems facing you.

If she knew about Hafiz and his attempts to undermine Isam, would she still have agreed to marry him? Or would she have been frightened off?

Isam thrust away the thought. With the determination born of confidence in his own abilities, he refused to worry over something that wouldn't happen. He'd overcome the plot against him.

Hafiz had acquired a taste for royal power and was doing his underhanded best to make people believe Isam's head injury had permanently affected his judgement and character. Today's problem with the timetable was part of that attempt. But he wouldn't succeed.

'It's been a big day and you're no doubt tired.' While Isam had to fit in several hours of work before he retired for the night. 'We'll talk tomorrow in more detail, but I'll announce our betrothal in the next few days.'

She jumped as if touched by a live wire. 'Days!'

He held her gaze, watching the gold flecks in her soft brown eyes. She was intriguing. Alluring. And his…almost.

'It's better for us to announce our news than for you to become the object of speculation, which will happen now your presence is more widely known.'

She didn't look convinced and it struck him that Avril

Rodgers was the antithesis of a gold-digger. She seemed uninterested in his money and his authority, much less the idea of becoming Queen.

He smiled. Perhaps this was cosmic justice for his casual arrogance as a much younger man. He'd been so certain of his desirability, given the number of women who had chased him, eager for attention and to bask in the reflected glow of his wealth and power.

'But once our engagement is announced, we can take our time planning the wedding. You'll have plenty of time to prepare for that.'

The question was whether he could wait that long to claim her.

Two days later, Avril stood in the centre of her sitting room while two seamstresses inspected the fit of her new gown. She couldn't think of it as simply a dress. This made-to-measure, one-of-a-kind garment was made from rich crimson satin that, when she moved, revealed a sheen of deepest amethyst. She looked from Bethany's approving grin from where she sat with Maryam on her lap, to the vast, gilt-edged mirror that had been brought into the room.

The woman reflected there bore only a passing resemblance to Avril Rodgers. Her hair had been professionally styled up in a way that looked stunningly elegant. Her equally professional make-up was discreet except for the crimson of her lips that matched the colour of her dress. The make-up artist had done something that emphasised her eyes, making them look…beautiful.

Avril had never felt beautiful before. She had favourite clothes that made her feel good and gave her extra confidence. But this was a transformation.

The red dress had tight three-quarter sleeves and a V

neckline. It was demure yet the neckline sat wider than usual on her shoulders, presumably to mirror her fitted bodice that tapered to her surprisingly narrow waist. She hadn't realised until today that she'd lost the rest of her pregnancy weight. Below her waist the rich satin skimmed her hips then fell in gleaming folds. The skirt was full and feminine and every time she moved the brush of the fabric felt like a caress.

You're thinking about Isam again. Stop it.

That was difficult, when even the slide of warm water down her body in the shower made her remember his touch.

Avril firmed her lips. Though he'd begun to remember her, he hadn't remembered intimacy between them, only work. He recalled her as his PA, nothing more.

What did that say about his priorities and her importance in his life?

She knew what it said. She'd never been more than a temporary lover, soon forgotten. She'd known that at the time, he'd been upfront about it. And she'd told herself it didn't matter. Yet *now* it mattered.

Avril remembered every word he'd said to her when he'd come for her answer the other day. He'd praised her quick thinking and pragmatism, qualities he'd wanted in a PA, and now apparently in a wife. There'd been nothing about him *wanting* her. Nothing personal.

When will you get it through your head? There's nothing personal between you any more. He's marrying you out of duty. Because of Maryam.

It had to be enough.

The seamstresses moved back and the designer, a sharp-eyed woman with silvery hair, finally nodded. 'It is done. I hope you like it, madam.'

'I do. I never thought I could look so—' Avril shook her head.

For the first time in their acquaintance, the older woman smiled. 'I rarely heed fashion advice from men. But I believe His Majesty chose well, insisting you'd be more comfortable in Western dress for the occasion.'

Isam had insisted? It was a small thing but it warmed Avril. She'd left everything to the designer, trusting she'd know best what would be suitable.

As if on cue a knock sounded at the door, a footman opened it and Isam swept in, resplendent in white, a heavy ring of old gold, symbol of royal authority, on his hand.

He stopped midstride, his robes swirling about his legs. Dimly Avril was aware of the women curtseying then following Bethany out through another door. She couldn't tear her gaze from the man who today would pledge himself to her. A royal betrothal was almost as binding as marriage.

Her heart pattered faster and her chest swelled on a deep breath. She watched his eyes widen then narrow as he surveyed her from top to toe then slowly, devastatingly slowly, back up.

Avril's flesh tingled. Her nape tightened and so did her nipples, thrusting against her new satin bra. Low inside, heat bloomed and muscles spasmed as if reliving memories of the night they'd been together.

He paced towards her, stopping only when he was so close she could smell the warm citrus scent of his skin and admire the close shave of his angled jaw. 'You look magnificent.'

His voice was husky, catapulting her back in time, making her remember how he'd made love to her, not just with his body, his mouth and hands, but with words of praise and enticement that had made her feel—

'Thank you, Isam. So do you. Every inch the Sheikh.'

She had to wrest back some control of herself. It was daunting enough to face an official photoshoot, knowing the photos would be pored over not only in Zahdar, but across the world. Isam was young to be Sheikh, handsome, talented and with a recent tragedy in his past. The world would be agog to see the woman he'd chosen as his bride.

A dreadful, plummeting sensation hollowed her belly. Was she foolish to think she could do this?

'What is it, Avril?'

She swallowed hard, tasting trepidation. 'I just…' She shook her head. 'How can you believe this will work? I'm not—'

Isam curled his fingers around hers and drew her against him. It was the first time they'd been so close since the night Maryam was conceived. The night he'd introduced her to a world of delight she'd never guessed at. A wonderful, golden world where anything was possible.

'It will work because we'll make it work. And you *are* everything you need to be.' Her gaze lifted to his, those grey eyes mesmerising and bright as liquid mercury. 'You're the mother Maryam needs and loves. You're talented, capable and caring. That's more than enough.'

The intensity of his stare made it hard to remember he wanted her for purely pragmatic reasons. Because when he looked at her like that she could almost believe…

Heat surged in her veins, bringing her skin to tingling life, flushing her throat and face. The way he looked at her, a huskiness in his voice she'd heard only once before, the words branding themselves in her brain… All those undermined her doubts and stripped bare her vulnerabilities. Made her hope.

Something cool touched her finger and she looked down

to see him hold a ring to it. He paused, as if waiting for approval or objection, then as she watched, he slid it home.

Her breath seized. The ring was remarkable. A huge crimson stone that she guessed was a ruby glowed with a dazzling inner light. Its setting was of old gold filigree that extended right up to her first knuckle. She blinked, trying to take in the delicately wrought flowers and…were those birds? She'd never seen such a thing.

It was a ring for a queen. A statement piece that spoke of extraordinary wealth and, she suspected, generations of tradition.

Daunting, much?

'I know in your country engagement rings are often chosen by the bride. But in mine they are usually an heirloom from the husband's family. I hope you like it.'

Avril swallowed, shaky at the grandeur and beauty of what she wore. It struck her that her dress was a perfect match for the stone, which was the perfect size for her finger. Had he organised it that way?

Of course he had. Isam was a man who saw details as well as the bigger picture. It was one of the reasons she'd enjoyed working with him.

'It's gorgeous but very grand. I'm not sure—'

'It was my grandmother's. I thought you'd enjoy wearing something from another bride who was an incomer. She was very happy in Zahdar and I hope you will be too.'

Avril looked up into his face, seeking a clue to his thoughts. She read tenderness when he referred to his grandmother but apart from that he wore his inscrutable expression. The one that left her second-guessing his thoughts.

He's probably wondering if you're up to the ordeal wait-

*ing for you now. At least it's better than him pretending
you're special to him.*

Finally she nodded. 'Thank you. That's very thoughtful.
I'll wear it with pride.'

And terror at the responsibility. But then it was so big
at least she'd know if she lost it.

There was a knock then the door opened and a voice
said, 'It's time, Your Majesty.'

Isam's eyes didn't leave hers. His voice dropped to a
low hum that resonated across her skin then settled deep
in the place where need was a twisting, hungry ache. 'It's
time. First the photos. Then to tell the world I want you as
my queen.'

He led her to the door before she had time to get even
more nervous.

The photo shoot wasn't as daunting as she'd expected. Just
one photographer and his assistant. The only difficulty was
smiling on cue.

Isam's words had thrown her into a tailspin. Avril welcomed his reassurance but when he'd spoken of wanting her
as his queen in *that* tone of voice, and with so much heat
in his eyes it should have made steam rise from her skin...

She'd almost believed he wanted her the way she wanted
him, with a dark craving that defied every attempt to squash
it.

He'd reawoken all that restless, useless longing inside
her.

She knew he meant that he wanted to marry her for
Maryam's sake. Because marriage was the simplest of their
options. So why look at her and speak to her that way?

He'd admitted he didn't remember being intimate and

she couldn't believe he was overwhelmed with desire for a weary, stressed new mum.

Unless it was a ruse to persuade her past her doubts. So she'd go through with today's announcement.

That had to be it. He'd wanted to spur her into compliance rather than have her cower in her room.

Avril lifted her chin, annoyed by such tactics.

'Perfect,' murmured the photographer. 'Just perfect.'

There was movement beyond him. Avril was surprised to see Bethany enter, carrying Maryam, who wore an unfamiliar, delicate gown of cream and gold.

Isam moved from Avril's side to scoop up their daughter. He turned and just like that Avril's heart forgot to beat for a second. Maryam smiled up at her father with wide eyes and he, broad shoulders curved protectively as he cradled her, wore an expression so tender it made emotion well.

Avril blinked and found herself softening.

She had no illusions that their marriage would be easy but it was the right thing for Maryam. She'd grow up with two loving parents.

'I thought we should include Maryam in some of the photos,' Isam said as he approached. 'Not for public consumption but for us.'

Avril nodded, throat tight at his thoughtfulness. In later years it would be something Maryam might treasure.

The man confounded her. One moment so caring, the next throwing her into utter turmoil.

It's not him that's the problem. It's you. You're an emotional mess. You want a man who can't remember being intimate with you. How can you expect deep feelings from someone who doesn't even know you?

Yet it was easier now to smile for the camera since the photographer didn't need posed shots. In fact, she was barely aware of him as Isam placed their baby in her arms, then settled beside her, offering Maryam his finger. Instantly their little girl grasped it and chortled.

Avril felt a rush of delight, aware of Isam's body warm beside her, his focus on their daughter, and Maryam's joyful response.

Yes. This.

They might have been brought together by circumstance but they could be a successful family unit, united in their love for Maryam.

They could do this.

Isam led her from the room towards the grand public reception spaces on the other side of the palace.

Were her nerves obvious? Isam glanced at her as the corridor widened and the furnishings graduated from luxurious to overtly opulent. Her heart was in her mouth at the idea of being presented to a bunch of VIPs as the country's next queen. Even his steady calm couldn't prevent the butterflies whirling in her stomach. Because of her confused feelings, or the ordeal ahead?

'It's a small reception. You'll be fine,' he murmured, his fingers tightening around hers. 'Pretend it's a business meeting, or a stray group of elderly petitioners come to tell me how to improve their lives.'

'If only.' She turned her head to see his encouraging smile. He was doing what he could to make this easier.

Even lie about wanting her?

Staff opened enormous carved doors and they stepped into a vast room with walls that looked like fields of beautiful flowers. Above soared a ceiling of gold from which hung rows of glittering chandeliers. And below that, a throng of people, all bowing low.

'A *small* reception?' she whispered as she faltered on the threshold.

'A mere two hundred. Tiny by royal standards.' Isam's mouth crooked up at one corner. 'Just be yourself, Avril, that's all you need to do. I'll be with you.'

He led her into the crowd that parted for them. Avril was aware of curious, assessing gazes and then bowed heads as their sheikh approached.

Except to one side where an older man walked swiftly towards a young woman dressed in silver, his expression thunderous. That look and the urgency of his gestures as he spoke to her struck a jarring note, especially as his narrowed gaze was fixed the whole time on Isam.

Beside Avril, Isam stiffened, but he kept his pace unhurried.

Someone stepped up to the podium. She recognised the minister whom she'd co-opted to provide refreshments for Isam's elderly guests.

His speech was short and ended in a burst of enthusiastic applause from the crowd that now encircled them. Then the minister spoke again in English, presumably for Avril's benefit. He announced the Sheikh's betrothal to Ms Avril Rodgers. To her surprise he added that they had a baby daughter and that mother and child were now living in the palace prior to the wedding. Then he concluded by wishing them well.

Another round of applause erupted and people surged towards them. For a second she hovered on the brink of light-headedness, feeling overwhelmed. Until Isam squeezed her hand and murmured that they'd do this together.

Strange how easily that settled her nerves.

She saw a single movement away from them, the scowling man striding for the exit. Then all her attention was claimed by well-wishers. Many had an air of gravitas as if very aware of their importance and many wore obviously expensive clothes, but all seemed genuinely pleased about the engagement.

It surprised her, as had the fact Maryam had been mentioned in the speech. Avril had supposed a foreign bride, who'd borne a child out of marriage, would be frowned on. Perhaps the Zahdaris were too polite to show disapproval.

Then her doubts fled as a familiar figure appeared. The tall, upright form of Hana Bishara, the woman Avril had met several days earlier.

Hana bowed to Isam then to Avril. 'I'm so delighted by the news of your betrothal. I can see our sheikh has chosen his bride well.'

'Thank you so much. It's lovely to see you again, Hana.'

The lady's smile widened. 'You remember my name?'

Avril grinned back at her. 'You were the first person I tried to speak to in Arabic. You were very encouraging and didn't even wince at my pronunciation.'

Hana laughed. 'Your pronunciation was admirable. Perhaps we'll meet again and you can practise with me.'

The friendly offer and the warmth of her manner cut through Avril's anxiety. 'Thank you. I'd like that very much.'

'I'll look forward to it too. But for now I must move on. There are others waiting to meet you.'

There were. To Avril it seemed like far more than two hundred but the short interlude with Hana had given her the boost she needed. Besides, everyone was friendly. She wouldn't be surprised if their smiles hid surprise or doubt, but she was thankful nevertheless.

Until she turned to find a woman in silver bowing before Isam. She'd been with the older man who'd left so abruptly.

The woman wasn't precisely beautiful but had presence, an elegance and confidence Avril envied.

Did she imagine a lull in conversation around them as the woman spoke to Isam then turned and wished Avril well in English?

Who was she? Avril thanked her, wishing she'd caught her name, before turning to the next person in line.

After that everything went smoothly. Buoyed by the warmth of her welcome and Hana's encouragement, Avril even began using her basic Arabic to welcome and thank the well-wishers. Which led to more smiles and nods of approval.

Beside her, Isam looked proud and regal but his manner was warm with his guests, even warmer when he caught her eye after it was all over.

'Superbly done, Avril,' he said as he led her back to the palace's private wing. 'Thank you.'

She shrugged. 'You were right. I didn't have to do much.' Even so she felt she'd run a marathon, her body only now beginning to relax. Yet having Isam at her side, a bulwark against nervousness, had made such a difference.

What does that say about your feelings for him? You're supposed to be marrying him for your child's sake, not because of some romantic fantasy you know isn't real.

Avril made herself concentrate on tonight's reception. She didn't delude herself that future events would be so easy. But it pleased her that she'd held her own. In fact she felt that buzz of excitement in her blood that she always got from a job well done. It left her wired and excited rather than tired.

Which had to explain her impulsive decision to invite Isam into her suite rather than say goodnight at the door. She wasn't ready for sleep. She had too many questions.

It had absolutely nothing to do with not wanting him to walk away. Nothing at all.

Avril watched him pace the room with a coiled energy that made her wonder if he felt the same high of excitement and satisfaction she did. Of anticipation...

'Why did you make the announcement about Maryam? Won't it shock everyone that you have a child? I thought you were just going to announce the engagement.'

Isam swung around, a lamp in the corner slanting light and shadows across his harshly beautiful features.

'You'd have me drip-feed the news? To what end? Our child is a cause for celebration.'

His delight stirred feelings she hadn't known she carried.

Because *she* hadn't been important enough for her mother or her father?

Was that the real reason she'd agreed to marry—because Isam clearly intended Maryam would be at the centre of his world? How could Avril resist that?

'Even so, we weren't married when she was born.'

His dark eyebrows drew together. 'In Zahdar we don't have such negative views about illegitimacy as in some places. Maryam will be welcomed here.'

He smiled. 'Besides, her existence proves we're compatible and fertile. One of the Sheikh's key roles is to ensure the succession, for the future safety of the country.'

Avril folded her arms, refusing to be amused. 'You mean they'll like me because I'm good breeding stock?'

That made her feel like a prize-winning sheep!

Isam paced closer. 'It doesn't hurt that we've produced a child. My father's early death was a shock, especially as I was badly injured. It made people wonder about the future and the stability of the monarchy.

'But tonight you showed the grace and strength I need

in a queen. People respect and admire that. They'll admire you even more when they get to know you. They'll approve my choice.'

He was doing it again, winning her over with flattery and that searing look, as if he wanted her as more than a convenient bride and mother to his child.

Avril took a step back, chin jutting. She couldn't play those games. 'I understand that. But I'd rather you didn't pretend to things you don't feel.'

She accepted theirs would be a real marriage. There'd be sex and maybe more children. In her secret heart of hearts, Avril looked forward to intimacy with Isam. But she didn't want convenient lies to salve her ego.

'Pretend?'

She looked down at her twisting hands. 'I appreciate all you're doing for Maryam, and to make our relationship appear solid. But I'd prefer you didn't pretend this is your *choice*. We're together because of circumstance, because of our baby, not because you *want* me.'

The silence following her words grew so long that finally she had to look up. Isam wore the strangest expression.

'You're right. Circumstance brought us together. Otherwise I'd probably marry a woman from Zahdar. Someone chosen for me in an arranged marriage. I—'

'Wouldn't that be hard to accept?' She reminded herself traditions were different here, especially for royals. 'You wouldn't marry for...?'

'Love?' His eyebrows rose. 'I believe my grandparents did but that was an exception. Here royal marriages are settled for dynastic reasons. That's the way for my family.'

He looked so calm, so matter-of-fact. As if the idea of marrying a stranger didn't bother him.

But then, that was essentially what he was doing with

her. She wished she could be so sanguine. To her it felt
wrong to marry for anything other than love.

Isam closed the gap between them, capturing her hands.
'But that doesn't stop me wanting you, Avril.'

CHAPTER TEN

ISAM LOOKED INTO SEARCHING, golden brown eyes and felt his control snap. His hands tightened on hers.

She thought he didn't want her?

He'd held back, needing to persuade her into marriage and not wanting to rush her physically. But he'd imagined his heated thoughts had betrayed him. After all, they'd been intimate before. He'd assumed she'd read his hunger, despite his attempts to rein it in.

But she was an innocent, remember? And you only had one night together. Maybe she's not adept at reading the signs.

The reminder that he'd been her only lover fuelled that renegade hunger, yet made him feel protective too.

He wrapped his arms around her and tugged her against him. A sigh chased its way up his throat as their bodies made contact.

Just holding her, fully clothed, made him shudder with satisfaction. What was it about this woman? She created a need in him more potent than any he'd ever known.

Her hands pressed to his chest, fingers splayed as she tipped her head back, keeping their gazes locked.

'You really *want* me?'

'Of course I want you. In London I broke every rule to

have you.' That he knew for sure. 'Since you came to Zahdar I've been having cold showers every day. I'm trying to give you time to adjust.'

She looked at him with solemn eyes. 'You never said.'

He frowned. Before the reception he'd told her he wanted her as his. But he'd been concentrating on reassuring her, supporting her in preparation for their first appearance together. Maybe he hadn't been completely clear.

'I'm saying it now. I'm desperate for you, Avril. Let me show you how much.'

Isam gathered her up in his arms and, when her lips curved into a fragile smile, marched across the room and into her bedroom, hitting a light switch on the way. He laid her on the bed, almost laughing at her expression of mixed shock and eagerness.

Despite her earlier doubt she didn't protest. Far from it. All the worries and demands of the long day disintegrated as he looked down at her, watching him avidly.

He wanted to take his time cataloguing everything from her velvet skin to the way the rich fabric enhanced her feminine shape. It was a hard-fought battle against the urgency that had tested him since meeting her across that London conference table.

Shucking off his shoes and keffiyeh, he followed her onto the bed, reaching for her foot in one jewelled sandal. Swiftly he released the narrow straps and tossed it away. He explored her instep, her dainty toes, high arch and curved ankle, registering each shiver and twitch in answer to his touch.

She was so responsive that he made himself pause rather than swiftly work his way up her body. He propped her heel on his thigh and worked the muscles of her foot in a deep massage. Her tension dissolved almost instantly. Her soft moan was the most erotic music.

It reminded him of the way she'd gasped out his name as she climaxed. *That* memory was clear and enticing and never failed to arouse.

Isam lowered her foot to the bed and stripped away her other sandal before massaging that foot.

Avril lay before him, fully dressed, eyes narrowed to slumbrous, golden slits, shifting needily, her hands curling into the bedspread.

A shaft of heat tore through him, settling in his already hard groin. He wanted her *now*, without preamble. But it would be even better if he took his time.

Her dress was soft as he pushed it up her legs, but not as soft as her flesh. Unable to resist, he pressed a kiss to her calf, then stroked it with his tongue, feeling her muscle spasm.

'Isam!'

Her voice was husky. It made his skin tight and weighted his groin so he had to take a moment, concentrating on control.

He looked up to find her propped on her elbows, watching him, eyes radiant with ardour.

'Patience, sweetheart.'

He wanted her so badly it hurt. But he wanted to imprint himself on her. To set up a deep-seated need in her that only he could assuage. To make her crave *him*.

Because he couldn't remember everything he needed to about how they'd come together?

Because that gap in his memory made him feel exposed?

He shied from that. Too often in the last year he'd felt that way. He preferred to take charge.

Isam wanted Avril, wanted sex, but he wasn't above

using their desire to bind her to him. She'd agreed to marry but he knew she still doubted her decision, and him.

He couldn't allow that. He had to make utterly sure of her. He'd give her time to acclimatise and prepare for the wedding, but having her back out at the last minute wasn't an option. Sex would reinforce the ties that bound them.

How delightful when duty and his own desire dovetailed.

You call this duty? You couldn't pull back from her if you tried.

Isam shoved the crimson skirt higher, pretending not to notice the fine tremor in his hands as he palmed her smooth thighs. Without stopping, he shoved the material over her belly, then stroked his fingers back down her hips, curling them into the pale lace of her panties on the way and dragging them down her legs. A second later they followed her sandals onto the floor and he knelt between her knees, gloating.

Avril was beautiful, more beautiful than he'd remembered. The contrast between her formal dress and her bare lower body only fuelled his excitement. He felt greedy and dizzy with anticipation. Like a teenager, teetering on the edge of control.

That he couldn't allow. He was determined to bring her pleasure before finding his own.

Slowly he slid his hands back up her thighs to her hip bones, not deviating to that V of dark hair, despite the way she twitched and turned, seeking his touch.

'Soon,' he promised. But first, he'd seen something else that fascinated him. The light caught striations low on her belly. His breath hitched as he guessed their meaning. 'Are they stretch marks?'

He'd heard of them but never seen any.

Avril shifted abruptly and Isam looked up to catch her

change of expression. Her eagerness had transformed into discomfort, her mouth forming a moue as if of distaste.

He frowned. To him these marks were a badge of honour, proof of her body's miracle in conceiving and carrying their child. Emotion welled at how special this woman was. How extraordinary.

He kissed the narrow lines and felt her stiffen. But he wasn't deterred. He explored each one, taking his time, telling her how proud he was, how thankful and how awed. In English and Arabic he praised her, telling her, with absolute truth, that he'd never wanted any woman more.

When he'd finished, her thighs were slack beneath him, her hands fisted in his hair and her eyes aglow.

His voice was thick and rough. 'You are so very beautiful, Avril.'

And she was *his*. He felt it deep in his belly, in the very marrow of his bones.

No other woman in his past had affected him like this.

Did she feel the same about him? The possibility that she didn't was unbearable. He wanted to bind her to him, not just with a promise of marriage but with ties of emotion and need.

He pushed her legs wide and settled between them, lowering his head. Her thighs trembled as he parted her folds to unveil that sensitive nub. Her whole body jolted as he captured it in his lips, drawing long and slow.

She gasped, her hands clenching tighter, holding him to her. As if he had any intention of leaving! The scent and taste of honeyed woman and arousal enveloped him and he couldn't get enough.

He needed to take his time, draw this out so that she hovered on the brink of bliss for as long as possible. But his own need weakened his determination. Instead of prolonging her pleasure he drove her further, faster, using his mouth and his hands until her quivering body rose desperately against him and shudders racked her. He felt her climax, tasted it, was part of it as she cried his name again and again, drawing him to her.

When he finally climbed higher to settle beside her Avril burrowed into his arms, her broken breaths hot at his throat, fingers clutching, legs tangled with his.

A tiny, thinking part of his brain triumphed at her response. But mostly Isam was caught in the pure joy of bringing her such pleasure. He wrapped her close, stroking her hair, delighted and possessive in equal measure.

Her eyes, when they opened, gleamed golden rather than brown and he felt something inside him soften and melt.

He wanted her to look at him like that again and again. He'd never tire of it.

Isam's already taut body stiffened with need as she moistened her lips to speak.

Then a wail pierced the night air.

Isam blinked, taking a second to identify the sound when all his thoughts had been on Avril and himself. It had felt as if no one else existed but the pair of them.

The sound came again, louder this time.

Avril slumped against him. 'Maryam.'

For a second he lay there, storing up every wonderful sensation, so much better than his broken memories of them together. Then, with a supreme effort, he rose from the bed and walked stiffly towards the cries.

A nightlight was on, giving the nursery a cosy glow. The baby looked up from the cot with a trembling chin, and tear-washed eyes. Before she could cry again he lifted her, rocking her gently. She didn't want to settle, instead mouthing the fine cotton of his robe.

'Sorry, little one. I can't help with that.'

But he could make sure she was changed and dry before taking her to Avril. When he returned to the bedroom with Maryam, Avril had changed into a cotton robe, sitting back against the pillows and smothering a tremendous yawn. She looked flushed and lovely though her gaze skated from his. Was she shy about what they'd done? Did she regret it?

Then she lifted her gaze from their daughter to him and her smile made something in his chest tumble.

'Thank you, Isam. I should have expected this.'

'What about the nanny?'

'I've told her I'd do the nights myself.' She shrugged. 'Maybe I shouldn't have insisted. It would be nice to get more rest, but she's been working all hours and deserved a break. Besides, I prefer my privacy. We close the door to her quarters at night.'

Isam nodded. He hadn't given any thought to their privacy as he'd set about seducing Avril. He'd been too caught up in his need for her.

That was a first. He couldn't remember any time when he'd been so lacking in caution.

Except when you got your PA pregnant.

What was it about Avril that made him forget everything else?

No time now to ponder. He carried the baby to Avril where she sat propped against the pillows.

Despite the colour in her cheeks and the glitter in her eyes, he registered the shadows of fatigue beneath those eyes. She covered her mouth as another yawn escaped.

It struck him how much had changed for Avril in a short time. She was a new mother in a foreign country where she didn't know the language or customs. She'd been brilliant tonight at the reception, but it must have been an enormous strain.

Isam had been working all hours, managing his royal responsibilities and dealing with crises that he believed were of Hafiz's making. As a result he'd barely focused on how daunting this was for her.

That had to change.

'It might be better if I leave you to finish up then get some rest.'

Her eyes rounded and she stopped in the act of opening her robe for the baby to feed.

'You're leaving?'

He caught her hand and pressed an open-mouthed kiss to her palm. He tasted honey-sweet woman and the salt tang of sex. A shudder of hunger ripped through him. One taste of her was nowhere near enough.

He swallowed, his voice rough. 'I want to stay. But if I do I'll be tempted to make love to you all night. I suspect you need your sleep now more than you need sex.'

'But you didn't…'

'Don't worry about me.' He hauled in a deep breath. 'Ever since we met again we've been working to *my* schedule, driven by *my* imperatives as King. Let me do this for you, Avril. Feed Maryam then rest. You look like you can barely keep your eyes open. Perhaps we can breakfast together.'

This time when Avril smiled, her pleasure had nothing to do with sexual desire, yet he basked in its warmth. It was the first real smile she'd bestowed on him since his accident. It felt like a rich gift.

Simply at the suggestion they share a meal.

You already knew she was unlike other lovers.

Yet that didn't explain his elation at her unguarded smile.

He kissed her hand again, inhaling the sweet essence of her, then made himself go to the door. He had to leave now or risk forgetting his good intentions. It was going to be a long night.

'Until the morning. Sleep well.'

'The food isn't to your taste?'

Avril started, her gaze locking on Isam's, and reaction rippled through her belly.

'It all looks lovely, thank you.'

She surveyed the food on the table between them, yanking her thoughts from last night. Difficult to do when her brain couldn't get past their renewed intimacy and the pleasure he'd given her.

The table was loaded with every conceivable breakfast item from fragrant savoury dishes to fruits, pastries, breads, dips, jams and even a large block of honeycomb dripping with sweet bounty.

'Do sheikhs eat like this every morning?'

He chuckled and even that set off reverberations deep inside as if she were attuned to him at a visceral level. 'I'm afraid I eat rather more frugally usually but I wasn't sure what you liked. Please help yourself.'

She nodded and reached for flatbread, cheese and a ripe fig.

It was hard to concentrate on breakfast when her mind kept returning to the magic he'd worked on her needy body. She'd been so sure they'd spend the night together yet he'd insisted on going, leaving her restless now despite the best sleep she'd had in months.

She'd been moved when he'd put her needs above his own. How many men would do that? Maybe there was a chance for her to become more than the bride foisted on him by circumstance.

Her blood sang and her appetite sharpened. She bit into warm bread spread with soft cheese, almost groaning with delight at its nutty deliciousness.

'You like that? Try it with rose-petal jam.'

His tone was husky, eyes glinting as he watched her eat. It was the same expression he'd worn as he watched her climax less than twelve hours earlier. He'd looked at her then as if *she* were the most delectable feast he'd ever tasted. The memory scrambled her brain.

Avril hurried into speech, needing something else to focus on. 'Tell me about the people at last night's reception. Who was the woman in silver?'

The woman had looked at the pair of them with the strangest expression, though her face had been bland when she'd approached and congratulated them on their engagement.

'Silver? Surely there were several.'

'She was with that man who behaved so oddly. You saw him too, he looked upset and he left without a word.'

Avril watched Isam pause in the act of helping himself to baked eggs. His abrupt stillness made her skin prickle.

She'd *known* there was something strange about the man, though the other guests hadn't noticed. They'd been watching her and Isam.

Isam finished filling his plate. 'You really are observant. I remember that from when we worked together.'

Her pulse quickened. 'You remember more about us together?'

'Still not everything, but lots, including your initial interview.' He smiled. 'You were very impressive. And I remember almost all the days we worked together in London.'

Avril struggled not to feel disappointed that it was only their business dealings he recalled, rather than anything personal. Surely if their intimacy had been important to him he'd remember it.

To Isam she'd been only his PA. Now she was his necessary bride. Never someone he wanted for her own sake.

Don't even go there. You need to keep your feet firmly on the ground.

'So who was he, the man who left without congratulating us?'

She watched Isam sip his coffee before replying, his deliberate movements confirming her intuition that this was important. Had he been trying to divert her from her original question?

'His name is Hafiz and he's a distant relative. After my father died and while I was in a critical condition, the Royal Council appointed him as regent. He held that position until it became clear I'd live, and then for a while afterwards until I was well enough to rule.'

Isam spoke matter-of-factly, yet Avril's heart hammered high in her throat. She hadn't known there'd been any question about him surviving.

'You're really all right now?'

'Really. Except for some persistent memory loss that's gradually improving.'

Yet his smile didn't reach his eyes. She could only guess how frustrating amnesia must be.

'You don't like him, do you?'

His eyes widened with surprise. 'As a royal I've spent my life keeping my emotions to myself. But you read me too easily, Avril, better than most people.'

She said nothing, just waited. Finally he said, 'I hadn't wanted to tell you yet. You have enough to deal with.

This—' his gesture encompassed their palatial surround-ings '—takes a lot of getting used to.'

'I don't need to be coddled. I'd rather understand what's going on.'

His prevarication only heightened her concern. The Isam she knew didn't dither. He was quick to grasp problems and take action. Yet now he seemed reluctant to talk.

Finally he shrugged. 'There have been problems for some time. At first I wondered if they were my fault. That's the way it seemed, or at least the way it was made to seem.'

'I don't understand.'

Isam's expression hardened. 'Nor did I. I was convinced my memory loss was only for the period before and dur-ing the accident, not afterwards. Yet important errors kept being made, all stemming from my office, apparently lead-ing back to me. No real damage has been done…yet. But it's been a close-run thing and only because my staff are so dedicated and loyal. There have been whispers among the few who knew about my amnesia, that perhaps I wasn't up to the job of ruling after all. That I was unreliable, my brain too damaged to work effectively.'

A chill of premonition skated down Avril's spine. 'You think Hafiz is behind that.'

Isam nodded. 'Behind the rumours, and, thanks to you, I'm now sure he's behind the problems we've had.'

'Thanks to me? I haven't done anything.'

'But you have. The day you found that group waiting in the courtyard, you described the man who'd loitered nearby. The one who hurried away when you called him. Your de-scription fitted someone who'd already raised suspicion. He's a secretary in the palace with access to my office and he has a close connection with Hafiz. My personal staff have checked his movements over the past several months and his access to restricted information. We believe he engineered every crisis we've faced.'

Avril stared, her stomach churning. 'You mean leaving those people out in the heat was deliberate? That could have been disastrous.'

'Exactly. And because they were told I'd personally requested them to attend that day, some might make a case that it was my fault. That I'm undependable and make erratic, pointless decisions.'

'*Some* meaning Hafiz?'

'It sounds far-fetched but it's no joke. The crises we dealt with were initially to do with leaked confidential information that might affect key commercial negotiations and national security. Now he's stooped to threaten the health of innocent bystanders too.' His voice hardened. 'All because Hafiz has developed a taste for royal power. I think he hoped I wouldn't recover and the council might make him Sheikh.'

'That's appalling! Surely no one would take him seriously.'

Isam's mouth tightened. 'He tries to capitalise on the fact that prior to the accident my work for the country was mainly behind the scenes. He even tried to paint me as a playboy with no interest in governing, based on a few high-profile lovers years ago.' Isam shook his head. 'When I was young I was impatient of royal protocol, leaving most official public duties to my father. But we worked as a team. I've helped run the country for years.'

Avril struggled to take it all in. 'But he can't get rid of you, can he? You're well.'

'I am. The only way I can be removed as Sheikh is if I'm proven incompetent to lead. That *won't* happen.'

She surveyed his grimly set features and relief stirred.

The thought of Isam dethroned by a conniving rival chilled her. Not that she knew anything about Zahdari politics, but she knew him. He had immense vision, was dependable and talented, the sort of qualities a leader needed.

The shock of his revelation made her realise her earlier doubts about his motives said more about her than him.

'Don't worry, Avril. Now we've located the mole in the palace we'll be able to prove what he's up to.'

'And Hafiz? What was he doing last night?'

Isam's mouth flattened. 'I can't say for sure but the woman with him was his daughter.' He paused as if searching for words. 'In the months after my accident the Royal Council strongly urged me to marry. Everyone likes the idea of an heir to carry on the succession. Hafiz suggested his daughter as a suitable bride and I agreed to consider the possibility. He was looking at ways to shore up his links to the throne.'

Avril's breath clogged her throat, making her voice thick. 'But then you found out I'd had your baby.'

It was one thing for him to say he'd probably have married a woman from his own country if circumstances had been different.

But it was another to discover that wasn't theoretical, that there *was* another woman!

A sophisticated, elegant woman who looked born to the role of Sheikh's wife. Who'd do it more successfully than Avril ever could.

No wonder the crowd had hushed as the woman in silver offered her good wishes on their engagement.

Avril folded her arms, hugging them close to her body, holding in the sudden wretchedness churning her insides.

'Yes. From that moment there was no question of me marrying anyone else.' After a second he continued. 'I never agreed to marry her, Avril. Only to think about it. As for Hafiz's behaviour last night, I don't know. But only a very few people knew about our engagement in advance. Hafiz wasn't one. My guess is he was furious that his ploy to marry off his daughter to me failed.'

Warm fingers covered hers and squeezed. 'Don't worry. Soon we'll have proof of his machinations. His campaign against me can't succeed. And you can be sure I'll look after you and Maryam. Believe me, Avril, I take my duty very seriously.'

CHAPTER ELEVEN

Duty.

There was that word again. Until she'd met Isam it had never bothered her. She told herself it shouldn't now. She was glad he wouldn't shirk doing the right thing by their child. Besides which, he was clearly besotted by Maryam.

If Avril's parents had loved her more, if they'd been as committed as him to doing their parental duty, they wouldn't have left her behind.

Don't go there. You can't change the past. As for the future, your focus must be Maryam, ensuring she has the parental love and care you didn't.

Cilla had been a wonderful role model and taught her so much, loved her so dearly. But there'd always been a part of Avril ready to believe she wasn't enough, wasn't lovable, and that was why her parents found it so easy to leave.

Now the man she was about to marry reminded her their wedding was all about duty.

She pushed down burgeoning hurt, crushed it into a dark recess behind her ribs and slammed a lid down on it. She couldn't afford to feel hurt, not if they were going to make this work.

'Sorry, what were you saying?'

Isam had spoken but she'd been caught up in her thoughts.

But the time for regret and doubt was over. She had committed to this.

'I said we need to spend more time together.' Pale eyes held hers but she couldn't tell what he was thinking. 'Since we returned to Zahdar I've been putting out spot fires of Hafiz's making. But now we have a lead on how he's causing the trouble, I can step back a little, help you adjust.'

Avril tried to ignore her flutter of pleasure. 'What do you have in mind?'

'My staff will organise briefings for you on palace protocol, local history and customs, and so on. Useful things that will help you when you become Sheikha. But you won't just be taking on a royal title, we'll be building a marriage. We need to know each other better, trust each other.'

'You want to get to know me?'

'Is that so bad?'

'Of course not. It makes sense.'

Avril didn't know whether to be pleased at his sensible approach, or disappointed. It sounded as though he intended to schedule slots for her in his busy timetable. Would they do Q and As across his desk?

The difference between that and last night's encounter, when he'd buried his head between her legs and taken her to the stars, made her want to weep. She wished he'd gather her close and make love to her instead of sitting on the other side of the table.

She didn't know where she stood with Isam. Most of the time he acted like a polite acquaintance, but last night... All she knew for sure was that he saw her as key to claiming his daughter.

Avril looked away, reaching for a peach, rather than reveal disappointment that, despite last night's intimacy, he viewed their relationship as something to be planned.

'How do you want to do that?' She bit into the peach, its sweet lushness the complete opposite of their dry conversation.

His expression changed, so quickly she couldn't read his gleaming eyes before his features settled again into calm lines.

She'd give so much to see him raw and unguarded.

'Sharing breakfast each morning would be a good start, yes?'

She kept her tone non-committal. 'Yes, an excellent start.'

'And perhaps there are some things you'd especially like to see and do. After we marry we'll tour the kingdom and I can show you my country. But for now it will need to be things in or near the capital. What interests you?'

Isam's question stumped her for a moment. She'd spent so long fretting over practicalities, preparing for single motherhood, worrying what would happen if her salary dried up, learning to care for a baby. How long since she'd thought of things she'd *like* to do?

Not since Cilla persuaded you to make that list.

'Avril?'

'There are some things,' she said slowly, remembering Cilla's enthusiasm and her own over the catalogue she'd compiled. She'd done it for Cilla's sake but had found a genuine spark of excitement at the possibility of expanding her horizons one day. Before Isam and an unexpected pregnancy changed everything.

He leaned closer, his clean, citrus smell invading her nostrils and making her tremble. 'Go on.'

'I want to learn to drive. In London there seemed no point but I always wanted...'

'What did you want, Avril?'

His low voice thrummed across her flesh, teasing her so she blurted out, 'Travel. Adventure. To see and explore. I wanted to see the Northern Lights. Learn to navigate by the stars. Go hot-air ballooning. Waterski and scuba-dive.'

She clamped her mouth shut. Adventure and a life of royal duty were hardly compatible. The only thing on her list that she was likely to achieve was to learn another language, not as she'd imagined—to help her on her travels— but simply so she could communicate in her new country.

To her surprise Isam grinned and despite everything she felt a ripple of pleasure deep inside. He looked jubilant, the habitual gravity of his expression morphing into an enthusiasm that made him look younger and stunningly handsome. Her pulse quickened and she leaned closer, drawn by his magnetism.

'You've come to the right place. Not for the Northern Lights, but we can travel to see them some time. For the rest, Zahdar is perfect. Along the coast there are some excellent diving spots and there's a lagoon perfect for waterskiing. Hot-air ballooning is popular inland and as for navigating by the stars, that's a highly prized local skill. Astronomers come from around the world to see our night skies in the desert. We have an excellent observatory. I can show all that to you, Avril. And I can teach you to drive.'

'*You* can?'

He nodded. 'Who better? We'll take a four-wheel drive out of the city.'

'A four-wheel drive? I was thinking of something small.'

'Why not learn to drive something that will take you off road? It's more practical here and all the better when you want an adventure.'

His enthusiasm was contagious, but she couldn't allow

herself to be carried away. 'Are sheikhas allowed to have adventures?'

She'd assumed her new future would be hemmed in by strict rules about conservative royal behaviour.

'Why not? My father said…'

Avril watched Isam's expression change, his smile falter. She waited but he didn't continue and she had the feeling that instead of seeing her his gaze was inward-looking. What did he see?

She waited. Was it a memory? Something he'd only now recalled? Surely that was a good thing. Then she saw his forehead scrunch up and taut lines bracket his mouth as if he were in pain. His hand went to the scars near his temple where his pulse throbbed.

'Isam.' She leaned in, her hand on his arm, feeling his tense muscles. 'Are you all right?'

She was used to him being strong and in control. The sight of him frozen in what looked like pain made her heart squeeze.

Finally, to her relief, he seemed to focus again. He stared as if surprised to see her.

She poured water into a crystal goblet and took it around the table to him, crouching beside him and curling the fingers of his other hand around the stem. Surely she only imagined they felt cold.

'Drink this.' She supported his hand, lifting it to his mouth. 'You'll feel better.'

She had no idea if it were true, but she couldn't bear seeing him like that. He sipped then lowered the goblet.

'My apologies.' His voice was a husk of sound and his throat worked as if he tried to coax stiff muscles into action. 'I…'

'Don't apologise. Are you okay?'

He rubbed his temple, frowning. 'I'm fine, nothing to worry about.'

But Avril did worry. Because despite all the warnings she'd given herself, Isam mattered to her.

Not because of Maryam or public expectations that they marry. But because she cared.

Even when they were boss and PA, when he should have been off-limits, she'd felt so much for him. It should be impossible, given how little time they'd spent together, but something about this man called to her. Made her yearn. Made her feel...

'Shall I call for a doctor?'

'No doctor!' He drew a deep breath. 'Thanks, but it's all good.' His mouth hooked up in a crooked smile that tugged at her heart. 'It may not look it but it's true. Sometimes memories come back easily and other times...' He rubbed his temple then reached for his coffee.

'It will be cold now.' She rose to her feet. 'I'll get a new pot.'

'No.' Long fingers shackled her wrist, warm and strong. 'Water's fine. Please, sit down. I don't need caffeine. I've already had enough stimulation.'

His mouth twisted wryly yet Avril saw the sheen of moisture brightening his eyes and knew he was more affected than he pretended. She covered his encompassing hand with hers.

She wanted to quiz him but he was entitled to privacy. They'd been physically intimate but not emotionally. It wasn't as if they...

'I'm sorry I worried you.' He took another long draught of water, his gaze fixed in the distance. 'I've been remembering more and more lately, but mainly less significant things. Now, out of the blue, I remember talking with my father on the day he died.'

Isam turned and fixed her with that turbulent grey gaze, heavy with emotion.

Her chest squeezed. Was he remembering the accident? 'Oh, Isam.'

'It's okay.' He moved his hand, threading his fingers through hers. 'It's a *good* memory, from before the crash.'

Yet her heart went out to him. Though she'd been prepared for it, Cilla's death had left her distraught. How much harder to lose a loved parent suddenly?

'I'm glad. Good memories are to be treasured.'

'He was particularly happy that day. I'd agreed to stand in for him so he could have a week off. He'd planned a couple of nights in the desert with a few old friends. I ribbed him about getting too old for camping and he said that a little adventure now and then was good for the soul. That it was important to take a break occasionally from the stress of governing.'

'He sounds like a wise man.'

Isam's eyes met hers. 'He was. The best man I knew.' He paused and she wondered if he was reliving that precious memory. 'He was pleased for another reason too, something else I've just remembered. I'm glad I could tell him that day.' Isam's voice roughened. 'That he knew before he died.'

Avril heard his raw emotion. 'You don't have to tell—'

'I want to.' Eyes that before had been pewter-dark now shone silver. 'Besides, it's related to your old job, my investments in Europe. Given everything else, I haven't had time to go through all the reports in detail.'

Her curiosity rose. 'Your business is doing very well.'

'Yes. So well that I told my father that day that I was in

a position to invest some of the profits. There was an initiative I wanted to start in Zahdar. When I'd initially raised it my father liked the idea but said other matters took priority, like funding medical facilities, infrastructure and schools. He wouldn't divert public money into it when there were too many other areas of need.'

Understanding dawned. 'So you decided to invest your private funds to raise money for it?'

He inclined his head. 'It will be a long-term project but it's important to me. I'd floated the idea with members of the Royal Council. Most liked it but Hafiz was against it, said it showed my priorities were wrong.' He frowned.

Avril broke the growing silence. 'I'd back your priorities over his any day.'

A smile tugged at the corners of Isam's mouth and the look he gave her made something inside sing.

'Thank you, Avril. When I was recuperating he'd mention things I'd apparently said or done that seemed to make no sense. For a while I wondered if my faculties *had* been affected by the accident. Before I realised he was trying to gaslight me.'

'He sounds like a poisonous man. I wouldn't trust him.'

'On that we're agreed. No doubt when I announce my initiative he'll try to undermine it.'

'But what *is* it?'

'It was inspired by my sister, Nur. You know she died young?'

Avril nodded, watching his expression cloud. Clearly his grief was still profound, both for his father and his sister. She thought of losing Cilla and what a relief it had been to talk about her aunt with friends rather than bottle up her loss.

'Was it a long illness?'

Isam's expression sharpened and she feared she'd said the wrong thing. Would he see this as prurient curiosity? For a long time he didn't speak. But eventually the words came.

'I was at home the night Nur became ill. She'd complained of a headache so I got her pain relief and sat with her while she rested. But when she opened her eyes a little later she winced at the light and she had a temperature, so I called the doctor.' He paused, swallowing, and Avril felt his pain. 'By the time he arrived she was complaining of a stiff neck and her temperature had spiked. It was meningitis, swift and fatal.'

Avril heard the desperation in his voice, saw him turn rigid, felt his hand tense around hers.

Not just with grief, she realised, but with guilt. Her heart ached for him. He had such drive, he was used to solving problems and making things better for people. How it must have hit him to be helpless to save his sister. No wonder he was distressed.

'I'm sure the medical staff did all they could.'

Isam inclined his head but his features remained strained.

'*You* did all you could, Isam. You were there for her, *with* her. You got help as soon as you realised there was a problem.'

'If I'd realised earlier—'

'How could you, when it just seemed like a headache? I'm sure the doctors told you that.'

He nodded but said nothing and she wondered if there was anything she could say to ease the burden. 'What was she like? Do you want to tell me about her?'

She saw his shoulders ease down. 'From the time she could walk she was always on the move. Most of the time she ran rather than walked. She was happy and curious, always busy, often laughing, and she had a kind heart.'

Isam's mouth formed a crooked smile that tugged at Avril's heart. 'She sounds lovely.'

'She was.' He paused and rolled his shoulders back. 'Nur was enthusiastic and energetic but sometimes found school difficult. She passed all her subjects but teachers expected much more and some of her peers were eager to see her fail.'

Avril must have voiced her dismay because he squeezed her hand. 'Sometimes being royal isn't easy. My father could have had her taught privately but he thought it important that she learn to mix with others and hold her own.'

Avril's respect for his family grew. 'That sounds tough.' Like most people, she'd thought of royalty mainly in terms of wealth and privilege, not its difficulties.

'Nur was athletic and sport became an outlet for her. She found her niche in team sports. She was a born leader, encouraging other players, building bonds between them. It was marvellous to see and all the girls gained confidence and abilities from what they learned together.'

'She was lucky to have such a proud big brother.'

Isam looked startled, then shrugged as if it was nothing. But Avril knew many children didn't have such loving support, and how much difference it could make, having someone who cared.

'You have to understand we don't have a strong history of female sport here. Sport isn't included in our school curriculum for either sex. That's what I want to change, to give them all the chance to participate no matter where they live or what their gender. Health experts and educators talk about the benefits of physical activity, and from watching Nur and her friends I saw so many positives. Not just fitness but self-confidence, teamwork, discipline and, for some, a chance to excel.'

He spoke so eloquently, it was easy to read the strength of his feelings as well as the work he'd put into exploring this. She felt caught up in his enthusiasm.

'I want to establish facilities across the country so all our young people have the chance to engage in sport, in school and outside it. I want to tie it into programmes on healthy living and give every child and adolescent chances simply to enjoy themselves. Life can be short and for some it's very difficult. This is another way to bring people together, building bonds and individual benefits.

'Sorry, I'm on my soapbox. It's something I want to do in Nur's memory. My father was fully behind it, if I could raise the funds.'

Avril sank back, moved by his passion. For his beloved sister and his people. How many political leaders used their own money to achieve something for the public good?

'I think it's a terrific idea, giving chances to people who don't already have them.'

She imagined there were plenty of remote locations in Zahdar. She wondered if Hafiz's objection were solely because of the cost or because the project would specifically include females.

'I'm not particularly sporty but I used to play volleyball.' Before her hectic job with a previous employer cut into her free time. 'I joined to keep fit and I definitely felt healthier for it, but I loved the camaraderie most of all.'

She hadn't realised until now how much she'd missed it. She'd had less time for friends after that.

Abruptly she became aware she and Isam still held hands. She looked at their intertwined fingers. There was nothing sexual in their touch yet it felt...powerful.

This man evoked such strong feelings, far more than a sexual yearning. He'd moved her with his talk of his sister and father. It was clear Isam had loved them, that their loss still hurt.

He felt deeply. How that appealed to her. Imagine being loved so steadfastly.

Now he was truly letting her into his life, sharing his hopes and emotions. Excitement rose. He'd opened up in a way that made her wonder if their future might be brighter than she'd thought. Perhaps, in time, there was a chance…

'What are you thinking, Avril? Tell me.'

It wasn't a command, but that coaxing, velvet voice was irresistible. She looked up and felt a beat of something pass between them. Heat rushed through her. She felt it climb her throat and pool deep too.

She could blurt out her neediness. How much she wanted from him. She could fret over his feelings. Or she could follow his example and simply commit to what now felt right.

Because she loved him.

Amazing that she hadn't recognised it before.

'You're a good man, Isam. I know an unknown, foreign wife isn't an ideal sheikha. I know Hafiz and others will try to use that against you, but I'll do my best not to let you down.'

CHAPTER TWELVE

FOR THE REST of the day Isam battled a headache. He got them less frequently now but occasionally, when the flood of memory returned, pain came with it.

Pain because he was still healing? Or because the memories were bittersweet?

But he couldn't wish them away. The memory of that last morning, his father's ebullience at the prospect of his short vacation and at Isam's news that his initiative for Nur could begin soon... That was priceless.

Isam rubbed the back of his neck and rolled his shoulders as he sat back from the desk. He knew the real reason for his pain—guilt lingering beneath his grief.

Because he'd lost his family and hadn't been able to save them. Everyone, the doctors and his father, assured him he couldn't have done any more for Nur, yet the burden of guilt would always lie heavy.

Now his father was gone too.

Isam had been told he'd done everything conceivable to save his father and the pilot. There'd even been amazement that, despite the severity of his injuries, he'd managed to drag them free before the chopper exploded. Yet that didn't ease his guilt.

How could he alone have survived? Why him?

He felt as though he'd let them down.

An image of earnest brown eyes swam before him, dragging his thoughts from the past.

'I'll do my best not to let you down.'

He shook his head. As if Avril would ever let him down!

Technically he hadn't known her long. Their working relationship had lasted less than a year and they'd only been reunited a short time. But he knew, as surely as he knew the view from this window, that he could rely on her.

Employing her had been a masterstroke. She'd handled every task assigned her and far more with competence and integrity. She'd so impressed that he'd wondered, during that week they'd worked side by side in London, why she'd settled for an assistant's job, working remotely rather than aspiring to a more high-flying corporate job. He could imagine her managing her own enterprise.

He hadn't realised then that she'd curtailed her career to care for her aunt. That made him respect her more.

Now she was to be his wife.

His pulse quickened, excitement stirring. And not because of her sterling work qualities.

He wanted her with a blood-deep hunger that defied all past experience. Wanted her body and her rare smiles. Wanted the excitement that had shone in her eyes when she spoke of having adventures. Adventures that he, with his privilege, took for granted.

And he wanted her tenderness. He saw the way she looked at their baby and felt almost jealous.

The few times they'd been intimate were emblazoned on his brain and his body, leaving him needy.

With Avril everything seemed magnified. Every sensation, every feeling.

Was it because, since the crash, he was starting out

afresh? That previous relationships seemed faded and insignificant? Or was it, as he suspected, more to do with Avril herself? Something about the intense spark between them? A spark he had no name for.

Then there was the fact she was the mother of his child. Emotion blindsided him whenever he dwelt on the miracle of Maryam's birth and the debt he owed her mother.

He'd changed Avril's life and was asking her to take on even more. He knew she was up to the challenge. It wouldn't always be easy, especially in the beginning. She'd have to face down the doubters.

Isam resolved to do everything he could to ease her way, to influence those who could make her life easy or difficult. He'd strive to arm her with the skills and knowledge she needed. That had to be his priority.

He glanced at the computer and the stack of paperwork on his desk, awaiting his attention.

Never had he ended the day without completing his work. Yet he shut down the computer.

He needed to be with Avril. His surge of memory this morning had interrupted their time together so they hadn't finished their discussion before his secretary came to chivvy him to his first meeting.

His blood coursed heavily in his arteries.

Are you sure it's a discussion you want?

'Isam!'

Avril put down the book on Zahdari customs and culture, staring at the tall figure who'd let himself into the sitting room.

Her heart stuttered then accelerated so fast she felt light-headed as she rose from the sofa.

His jaw was shadowed and his thick hair slightly rumpled as if he'd run his hands through it. Even his scars looked rakish, accentuating rather than detracting from his charisma. His dark suit emphasised his straight shoulders and long legs. His tie had disappeared and his white shirt was open at the throat.

An invitation to touch, whispered a subversive voice.

'Who did you expect when you invited me in?'

'I thought you were a maid. From what your secretary said, I assumed you'd be working well into the evening.'

Avril watched him flex his fingers as if trying to ease tension.

Could it be the same tension she felt? It had drawn her to her feet, heart hammering as adrenaline pumped in her blood and heat pooled low.

Don't be stupid. He's here to discuss something pragmatic.

Maybe the full schedule of appointments she'd acquired today to meet dressmakers and various experts who would supposedly turn her into someone fit to be royal.

'I should be working.' His voice sounded strained. 'But I needed to see you.'

'Is something wrong?' When he shook his head she continued. 'You wanted to talk about another public appearance?'

'No. We do need to talk.' His voice was harsh and she watched him swallow, tracking the jerky movement of his throat and feeling something like triumph. 'But later.'

Avril waited but he seemed in no hurry to explain, merely stood there, watching her.

Isam moved from the door and the gleam in his deep-set eyes made her nape prickle.

Another step and another, slow, almost languid, yet there was a decisiveness in the set of his jaw and something in the flare of his nostrils that rooted her to the spot, excitement igniting. Her breathing shallowed and she felt the laboured lift of each quick breath as he closed the space between them.

Her heart had bled for him this morning as she'd witnessed his grief and joy at remembering his father on that last day.

This man had the ability to wring her heart but it was too late to retreat. For she'd already surrendered hers.

She'd feared that would make her weak but now, watching his absolute focus as he closed in on her, like a man drawn by a power he couldn't resist, she felt strong. Excited. Thrilled.

As if, for the first time, she was truly *seen*. Not as an employee or a complication. Not as someone he was duty-bound to acknowledge. Nor as the bride he felt obliged to claim.

As a person in her own right. A woman he couldn't relegate to a neat pigeonhole. A woman who got under his skin the way he'd burrowed under hers.

'Why are you here, Isam?'

She had a fair idea but she had to be sure. Her experience with men was limited.

Because no other man ever tempted you. No one else made you feel this way.

'I couldn't stay away.' He stopped before her and she angled her chin to hold his gaze. 'I've been trying to hold myself back and give you space and a chance to rest. Each day it's more difficult. And after last night…' He shook his head. 'I want you, Avril. I can't concentrate, can't work. I need to be with you.'

It was there in the tension honing his striking features. In the glitter of his eyes and the set of his shoulders. Avril felt it too, the ponderous beat of her heart and the melting between her legs.

'You want to have sex with me.'

Tiny vertical lines appeared in the centre of his forehead. 'Not just that but yes. Definitely, yes.'

If anything had been needed to banish last night's fear that he'd brought her to climax simply to make her more amenable, it was the sight of Isam now.

Avril's mouth curled into a smile that felt sultry with invitation. 'Yes.'

He blinked, pupils flaring dark in that sizzling stare, and for a moment there was utter stillness. Then his mouth curved in one of those devastating smiles that had always gone straight to her heart.

'Avril.'

Her name sounded like relief and joy. Acknowledgement and invocation. No one had ever turned her name into something so glorious.

His name formed on her lips but before she could speak he wrapped his arms about her, drawing her up against him and claiming her mouth.

His strong body and his embrace held her securely as her knees weakened. The taste of him, the urgency, undid her. The perfection of their kiss snapped the last ties of her self-control that had already been loosened by the realisation she loved him. How could she hold back?

She slid her arms up between them to lock her hands behind his neck, holding him to her as he dipped her back. There was a feeling of weightlessness, as if the world spun away, but she had no fear of falling from Isam's arms.

This was where she belonged.

Avril kissed him back with an enthusiasm born of old fears and new hope. She was ardent and clumsy. Far from minding, his low growl hummed with approval. And was that possessiveness? Her heart leapt.

'The nanny?' he murmured against her lips.

'Gone for the night.'

Isam lifted one hand to cup her jaw, the weight of those long fingers branding sensitive skin. Fire trailed from her throat to her breasts, her nipples budding. Even the scratch of skin against bra felt arousing.

'The baby?'

Avril turned her head, catching his thumb between her teeth and biting down. His gaze heated and she felt the fire in her breasts arrow straight to her pelvis.

'Asleep,' she mumbled against his thumb. He tasted better than anything she knew. 'I just put her down.'

His chest expanded hugely, pushing against her swollen breasts as he drew a deep breath. 'I need you, Avril.'

She speared her fingers up to clasp his skull. Even the sensation of thick hair against her hands was an erotic assault, making her quiver with need. Her breathing was almost a pant as desperation rose.

'I need you too.'

There, she'd said it. Instead of weakening her, the admission felt like triumph. Because whatever she'd feared, there was no mistaking Isam's hunger for her. It didn't take the impressive arousal hard against her belly for her to realise he was on the edge of control.

Isam straightened, one arm around her waist and another around her buttocks, lifting her clean off the floor. The proof of his strength only turned her on more.

Their mouths met again, not so neatly this time, clashing a little in their desperation. But Avril wouldn't change a thing. She preferred raw and real to any practised seduction.

Their first night together had been wonderful. But this

was on a new level. Despite his strength she felt tremors running through his big frame as if he struggled against a force too powerful to withstand.

'Need a bed.'

His muffled words fell into her mouth, another aphrodisiac, and she feared she couldn't take much more.

'Why not here?'

Avril felt his body jolt. His mouth lifted just enough that he could hold her gaze. She stared straight back then deliberately arched, pressing her aching breasts against his chest.

He whispered something that might have been a prayer or a plea and then he was moving, striding across the room until her back met the wall. He held her there, pressing her with the weight of his tall frame.

His arm around her waist slid free so he could cup her breast. Her eyes shuttered as she pushed into his palm, at the same time registering the thrust of his thigh between hers. Instantly her legs parted, allowing him to wedge himself against her so she was caught between him and the wall.

Sensations bombarded, inciting a voluptuous shudder.

'Isam. I need—'

'Yes. Me too.'

Avril opened her eyes and drew her hands around to his face. Tenderly she traced the web of scars that ran into his hairline, her heart overflowing at the idea he might have died.

She stroked lower, hearing the scrape of her fingers on his scratchy jaw over the pounding of her heart. She spread her fingers to cup his jaw as she met his eyes and emotion filled her. 'Can we? Here?'

There'd never been a sexier sound than Isam saying,

'We can and will,' in a baritone growl that reverberated through her chest and right down into her feminine core.

Relief soared as together they tackled his belt and zip. Seconds later her hand closed around firm male flesh and her internal muscles clenched needily.

Callused hands skimmed up her legs, pushing her dress to her hips. A second later knuckles brushed her splayed thighs and fingers hooked around her underwear. One tug brought the sound of tearing fabric and her eyes rounded. Avril wondered if it was possible to climax just from anticipation.

Did Isam read her thoughts? Obviously he read her body because that tiny knowing smile reeked of male smugness.

In answer she slid her hand the length of his erection.

She would have laughed as his smile disappeared and he swallowed abruptly. But there was no joking now, only a compulsion to mate. As if she'd die if she couldn't have him.

'Avril.' The single word held all the longing that filled her.

'Yes, now.'

He touched her again and she tilted her pelvis, hungry for the contact of slick flesh against clever fingers.

Isam eased her hand away from him then lifted her leg, hooking it around his hip. Eager, she raised the other with his help and locked her ankles, encircling him. She was wide open to him, and unbearably excited.

Gently he lifted her higher against the wall and when she slid down a little there he was, waiting for her, probing soft flesh.

Even that felt almost too excruciatingly arousing. She needed him, all of him.

Hands on his shoulders, she bore down just as he thrust up. A lightning flash of silver heat. A precarious moment of stunned disbelief as their bodies met in perfect harmony. The nagging hollowness filled with proud virility. Hardness melded with softness, need with need.

They hung together, suspended on the edge of perfection. Then, as if their twin bodies responded with exact synchronicity, they moved together. Friction deepened perfection. Sensation heightened to awe. Until it became too much and pure joy consumed them.

Avril lost herself in the grey eyes of the man who'd stolen her heart.

It felt as if she glimpsed paradise.

'We do have things to discuss, Avril.'

They were fully dressed again though she knew she must look rumpled. She *felt* rumpled, her dress creased, her body quivering with sensual after-shocks and her brain dazed with delight.

How she wished they'd moved straight to the bedroom after that exciting coupling. The last thing she wanted was to talk about the world beyond these rooms and all the daunting responsibilities she faced.

Sated as she was, Avril hadn't been ready to end their sexual encounter. She wanted to lie naked in his arms with the freedom to explore his superb body. Perhaps tempt him into another erotic venture. He'd opened the doors to a world of sensual fulfilment and she had so much catching up to do.

In contrast Isam, sitting beside her on the sofa, looked as vibrantly handsome and centred as when he'd walked in. As if he'd strolled into her sitting room for a business discussion.

She resented that. He'd swept her away on a tide of passion and she wanted to linger there. In that blissed-out place she could pretend, for a little while, that she was precious to him, that what they shared *meant* something.

She suppressed a sigh. It *did* mean something. That he was still attracted to her physically.

Avril's mouth tightened. Since they were going to marry that was a good thing. Even if he wasn't emotionally engaged, they'd have a satisfying sex life.

She ignored the voice screaming silently that it wasn't enough. It *had* to be enough, for her sake and Maryam's. Avril would care for her daughter as her parents hadn't cared for her. Even if it meant—

'Did you hear what I said, Avril?'

'Sorry. I wasn't really concentrating.'

She looked across and met his surprised stare.

Obviously he was used to holding his audience's attention. One of the prerogatives of being royal.

But as she remembered him this morning, grieving and vulnerable, her indignation disintegrated.

Avril wondered if his determination to accept and raise Maryam had roots in his feelings for Nur. He'd lost the people closest to him. Now he was determined not to lose the tiny girl who was his only family.

Her heart turned over, as she thought of the lengths he was going to for Maryam's sake, courting scandal and bringing in an unsuitable wife.

It wasn't Isam's fault he didn't love Avril. He was doing his best. And from what he'd told her about the situation with Hafiz and his own recovery, doing it under incredibly difficult circumstances.

Her voice softened. 'What is it, Isam? What did you want to talk about? Is it my next public appearance?' She repressed a shiver of trepidation.

'That's important, but for now we need to agree on something more urgent.' He covered her hand with his. 'More personal. I want us to live together, now. I see no point waiting to marry.'

'Live together?'

The smile forming on his face faded. 'Why not? After last night and tonight, I know you're as eager for intimacy as I am.' Before she could respond he went on. 'I see the shadows under your eyes, Avril. If we spend the nights together I can help share the burden of looking after Maryam.'

'You want to help look after the baby, hands on?' She recalled that he'd helped care for his sister but despite his assistance last night he surprised her. 'Surely you're already carrying enough of a burden with your official responsibilities?'

His fingers firmed around hers and the hint of a frown carved his forehead. 'I want a real relationship with my daughter, not just to see her for half an hour between meetings. My family is as important to me as my country.'

His family. He meant Maryam, not her. Avril forced down a sigh, refusing to wallow in self-pity. She was grateful he felt such a strong bond with their daughter.

'I'm not arguing, Isam. I'm just surprised. I was thinking of potential scandal. I imagined people wouldn't approve if we were—'

'Sharing a bed?' His chuckle ignited a flare of feminine arousal that made her shift on the seat. 'I'm sure people assume that's exactly what we're already doing. They'd be surprised to know I haven't been regularly bedding the beautiful mother of our child.' His level stare told her he was serious. 'As to scandal, we've already done that. An affair and a baby born outside marriage.'

It was as she'd suspected. 'Will that play into Hafiz's hands?'

Isam raised his eyebrows and she glimpsed hauteur in

his proud, uncompromising features. An arrogance that startled her, reminding her he was the hereditary Sheikh, born to power. A man used to succeeding and winning what he wanted, no matter what the odds.

'Don't worry, Avril, I have his measure. He won't succeed. You and I have had an…unconventional relationship so far but that doesn't matter. People are pleased about our baby and delighted at our upcoming marriage.'

Because they wanted their sheikh to provide an heir. Not because they approved his choice of bride.

He was sparing her feelings but she suspected there must be a lot of negativity about her, despite her proven fertility. Her lips twisted, because that was her real value in this equation. Her ability to provide an heir to the throne.

Warm fingers curled under her chin, raising it so their eyes met. She saw warmth there and something that made the tightness within her unfurl. 'There's nothing for you to worry about, Avril. I promise.' He paused and for a moment she almost thought he looked nervous. But Isam didn't do nervous. He was the most confident, capable man she'd met. 'You still haven't answered me.'

'What was the question?'

He leaned in. 'Us. Living together. Now.'

Avril licked suddenly dry lips and saw his eyes track the movement. Heat bloomed across her flesh as his eyelids grew heavy in a look of sultry expectation that opened up an emptiness in her pelvis. Her breath was a shuddery sigh. He only had to look at her that way and she turned to mush.

She feared the power he had over her, the strength of her own yearning. The desperate desire to blurt out a *yes*.

But why hold back? She wanted intimacy, wanted to build a family with him and Maryam. Wanted Isam.

'Yes.'

Her mouth was still forming the word when he leaned across and scooped her up onto his lap. 'Excellent.' Then he smiled and the devil was in his eyes. He rose, holding her effortlessly against his chest. 'Come and tell me what side of the bed you'd like to sleep on.'

But as he carried her to the bedroom she knew it wasn't sleep on his mind. Anticipation fired her blood.

CHAPTER THIRTEEN

AVRIL HURRIED TO put on her make-up. She'd been distracted, playing with Maryam.

At six months, her little girl was such fun, babbling happily and blowing bubbles. She could roll over now, reaching for her toys, and sit up with only a little assistance.

Isam, an adoring father, insisted she was gifted. Avril was just happy Maryam was thriving. Seeing her with her father confirmed Avril was doing the right thing.

So why did the fact the wedding was mere weeks away create a chill deep inside?

Avril ignored the sensation, telling herself it was nerves before another royal event. They still made her edgy. She knew Isam took a risk, marrying her, an outsider who had little to recommend her as Queen. As a result she worked hard to learn everything necessary to take her place at his side.

The last two months had been a roller coaster. Intimacy with Isam was even better than before, and there were times when she felt the connection strong between them. She often accompanied him to official events and it was getting less fraught each time.

She muddled through with his help and that of Hana Bishara. It transpired that Hana was a retired language teacher and she'd become Avril's tutor and friend. Through her Avril now knew a number of women, regularly meeting them for coffee afternoons. Gradually the sense of isolation began to ease and she knew that in time, if she worked at it, she could make a niche for herself here.

Avril put down her mascara and pressed a hand to her churning stomach, turning from the mirror.

Did she *want* to make a niche here?

In theory, yes. For Maryam. And for herself, since she would marry the man she loved. The man whose ardent passion turned their nights together into bliss.

Yet disquiet stirred. Despite her best efforts it was getting worse, not better.

On the threshold of the bedroom she paused and made herself focus on the beauty before her.

Isam had moved them into a different suite, one that had been his grandparents'. It was grand, as everything in the palace was, but something more too.

The walls of the bedroom were hand-painted to create a romantic bower. The wall behind the bed was a trellis of lush roses, so realistic it felt as if she could reach out and pluck one. The other walls depicted a beautiful spring garden and the rolling green hills of England.

His grandfather had presented it to his wife as a wedding gift, afraid his new bride might pine for her homeland. Isam thought Avril would like it too.

She did, enormously. But she couldn't prevent a poignant ache, wondering how it would feel to be so loved by a husband that he'd create such a romantic place for her.

Avril frowned, guilt stirring.

Isam was doing everything he could to make her feel at home. Teaching her to drive, his patience and encouragement making it easier than she'd thought.

There'd been private outings, just the pair of them, to places he thought she'd enjoy. An idyllic private beach where they'd swum and made love. A superb lunch high in a modern glass tower with a bird's eye view of the city, where he'd pointed out new developments and traditional parts of the city he loved so much.

One evening he'd taken her outside the capital for a supper picnic. Away from the city lights they'd gazed at the brilliant stars and he'd begun teaching her their names. They'd go hot-air ballooning after the wedding too.

Isam was thoughtful and kind, and his passion excited her. But there was something missing.

Unlike his grandfather who'd had these beautiful rooms decorated for his bride, Isam didn't love her.

Avril told herself it didn't matter. This was the best solution to their situation.

You want more than a solution. You want love.

The one thing she'd always craved.

She shook her head, discarding her robe and putting on the clothes laid out for her. The beautiful green dress and shoes had been custom made. Yet she barely registered their luxury. She was too busy telling herself, as she did daily, that she was doing the right thing.

She'd promised to marry and she would, for Maryam. And because she couldn't bear the thought of leaving Isam.

'Ms Rodgers, it's very kind of you to single me out again. There are so many who'd like to talk with you.'

Avril met the elegant brunette's eyes, reading pleasure there as well as tension. She felt sorry for Hessa, Hafiz's daughter, guessing how difficult public appearances must be. Word had got out that Hessa had been suggested as a royal bride but rejected by Isam. How many in the crowd also knew her father had plotted against his sheikh?

Even at this celebration to open Zahdar's new national library, Avril had seen the nudges and whispers.

She moved closer. 'Not at all. It's nice talking with someone of a similar age.'

'His Majesty doesn't mind?' Hessa looked past Avril as if expecting Isam to stride through the throng and separate them.

'Of course not.' On the contrary, he'd thanked her for talking to Hessa at a previous event, when others had treated her like a pariah. Avril suspected he felt sorry for her, tainted by Hafiz's behaviour.

'But my father—'

'You're not your father.' As far as Avril could see, the man had left his daughter to face public curiosity alone. He hadn't attended any public or royal events since the engagement announcement.

'You're very understanding. I'm so glad the trouble he stirred this week hasn't affected you after all. It would have been a shame.'

'This week?' Avril hadn't heard anything about him lately. Isam had told her things were under control with Hafiz.

'Yes, that incident in the marketplace and…' She shook her head, eyes shadowed. 'I apologise for his behaviour. It saddens me that he used you in that way.'

Avril was about to find out more but thought better of it. This wasn't the time or place. Besides, a tickle of awareness down her spine told her they weren't alone.

It was the sensation she got whenever Isam came close. Her body recognised and responded to his nearness even when she hadn't seen him.

Excitement stirred as it always did. She *wanted* his company. But there was something else too. A despairing ache that swamped everything else.

Despair because their months living together had confirmed what she'd feared. The love she'd recognised so recently was as potent as ever. It showed no sign of diminishing. Her emotions grew deeper as time passed. She was in his thrall, totally responsive and eager for him.

But to Isam she represented duty.

She doubted that would ever change. He was considerate and tender, passionate too, so passionate her toes curled thinking about it. And his love for Maryam…

Her heart clenched. He was capable of love, just not for her.

'Your Majesty.'

Hessa sank into a curtsey. As ever, Avril admired her grace. She was elegant, arresting, and knew so much about the country and its politics.

She'd make a much better sheikha than you.

A deep voice spoke. 'Hessa, it's good to see you.'

Isam reached out to take his wife's hand and felt the tiniest flinch. He watched her shoulders rise, a sure sign of tension.

Concern speared him. For the past few weeks, despite his best efforts, something had gone wrong between them. But what? Whenever he tried to broach the matter she changed the subject, telling him everything was fine.

Fine. Such a bland word. He didn't want to settle for fine.

Initially she'd seemed to enjoy being with him as much as he wanted to be with her. He'd thought they bonded over Maryam. They'd even shared the once familiar camaraderie that had characterised their working relationship. As if they understood each other, almost without words.

She'd never physically withdrawn from him before. On the contrary, her passion for him seemed endless. Even, of late, almost desperate. Now her composure seemed brittle.

He sensed her fragility.

Hessa spoke, drawing his attention. 'Thank you, Your Majesty. May I congratulate you on the new library? It's a stunning building and a wonderful resource, particularly for researchers.'

'I'm glad you think so.' He and his father had sponsored the project together and he was proud of it. He explained to Avril, 'Hessa is a historian and this building will house prized ancient texts and records as well as being a library for the general public.'

Avril immediately began asking the other woman about her work and the documents she consulted in her research.

Pride filled him. That Avril should make such an effort to put Hessa at ease when so many avoided her now. That showed a generosity of spirit that he admired. But it wasn't just Hessa. Avril happily engaged with everyone from VIPs to market vendors, treating them all with courtesy and interest.

Yet concern overshadowed his pride. Something was wrong and he didn't know what. It worried him, seeing her so on edge. Was Avril overwhelmed by her royal responsibilities? Or by the unfamiliarity of her new country?

Gently he squeezed her hand, signalling his support. But she didn't respond.

Anxiety stirred in his belly. Whatever problems they'd faced, she'd never been indifferent to him.

'It's time for the official opening.' His voice roughened. 'If you'd like to come and help me cut the ribbon, Avril.'

'Of course. This will be a first for me.'

Her lips curved into a wide smile. But it didn't reach her eyes. Her gaze was curiously blank and fear feathered his nape.

He needed to get to the bottom of this. Today.

Two hours later he followed Avril into their sitting room. Despite his worries, his gaze lingered appreciatively as she crossed the room, hips swaying because of her high heels. Her dress, fitted around the upper body and skimming her hips and thighs, was modest, except he couldn't help visualising her body beneath the gleaming silk.

His blood heated. Months living together had done nothing to assuage his need for her.

He struggled to focus on something other than his primal hunger for her. Calling on years of practice, Isam turned to assessing today's event. Avril had been a huge success and not just with the attendees.

Zahdar's fashion designers loved her, vying for the chance to dress her. It helped that she was gorgeous. But she also went out of her way to support local makers. That green silk had been manufactured by a new enterprise reinvigorating the old art of silk production. Even the pattern of the fabric was an advertisement for Zahdari design. The delicate white lilies grew in the mountains and were a symbol of his people.

'Isam. You're staring.' She brushed her hands down her skirt, inadvertently drawing attention to the swell of her hips and the line of her thighs. 'Is there something wrong with the dress?'

He shook his head and followed her further into the room, arousal stirring. But this wasn't the time for sex. He turned to pour them cool drinks.

'On the contrary. I was thinking it perfectly balances

support for local industry with chic style. I applaud you on your choice.'

She was stunning, beautiful and utterly sexy.

He opened his mouth to tell her then paused. So often she brushed aside his compliments on her appearance as if not believing him. On the other hand she was anxious about measuring up to her new role and liked feeling competent. That gave her confidence.

He held out a glass to her, trying to stifle disappointment when she took it without even a brush of fingers against his.

'Today was a resounding success, and you played a big part in that,' he said when they were both seated. Again Avril distanced herself, choosing a chair instead of the sofa they'd shared so often.

Another pang of disquiet arrowed through him.

'Thanks for your efforts with the head librarian and the mayor.' He smiled, remembering the way both men had responded to her attentive questions. 'I'd feared that, given their past differences, we'd have some awkward moments, bringing them together. But it worked out well with your help.'

Instead of looking pleased, Avril nodded and frowned down at her drink. Each day she seemed to withdraw further from him. Despite their physical intimacy, something had changed. Something that made her eyes sad when she didn't think he was looking.

He couldn't bear it. 'Avril—'

'Isam, I—'

'You first,' he said.

His expression was unreadable and Avril was worried. Despite his encouraging words she knew Isam had something weighty on his mind.

Was it the trouble she'd caused? Hessa hadn't given details but it was clear there'd been problems Hafiz had used as ammunition in his campaign against Isam.

'Why didn't you tell me?' She leaned forward. 'I had to find out from Hessa of all people that I'd done wrong.'

Isam frowned as if he didn't know what she was talking about. How much had he withheld? 'I don't know——'

'Don't, Isam. I know Hafiz used something I did recently, some *things* I did, trying to discredit me and, through me, you.' She looked at the glass grasped tightly in her hands and put it down before she spilled anything. 'You treat me like a child, not trusting me with the truth.'

'Hardly like a child!'

Heat blazed in his eyes, a combination of sexual awareness and indignation, as if he wasn't used to being called on his behaviour. Of course he wasn't. He'd been raised royal, trained to expect deference and obedience.

It was a side of him she didn't see often. But those occasional glimpses of innate arrogance, however tempered, were an important reminder of who he was. Sheikh first and foremost. Not her soulmate, however much she wished it.

'You withhold important information. How can I learn if I don't know when I've done things wrong? How can I feel confident I'm doing the right thing in public?'

The royal aspect of this new world was daunting. Yet she'd happily face that if she felt she and Isam were truly partners. Increasingly, however, she realised that was a pipe dream.

'There was nothing important——'

'You're still denying it. Why can't you be straight with me?'

Isam shook his head. 'I *am* straight with you. Despite

what you heard from Hessa, you didn't do anything wrong. It was just Hafiz trying to twist things.'

Isam sighed, scraping his hand across his scalp. In his dark suit, tie undone and hanging loose around his open collar, he reminded her of the vital, fascinating business-man she'd met in London.

Her heart squeezed as she wished, not for the first time, that he were just that, an ordinary man. For there was a chance an ordinary man might fall in love. But royals in Zahdar were immunised against that, taught from the cra-dle to expect loveless marriages.

Isam had so much love to give. She'd seen how deep his feelings ran for his sister and father, and she saw every day how much he loved Maryam.

But romantic love? He'd inferred romantic love wasn't for him. and Avril feared he was right. Even after every-thing they'd been through he was busy protecting her. He didn't see her as an equal, just a responsibility.

The enormity of what she faced overwhelmed her. She'd thought she had enough love for the pair of them. That she could make do with what he offered her.

Was she fooling herself?

'The main thing to know is that Hafiz wasn't success-ful.' Isam paused, as if making sure she digested that. 'He saw a video of you dancing at the community centre last week and spoke out about it in an interview.'

Avril frowned. She'd been at the centre with Hana and some of her friends, attending a women's afternoon. It hadn't been an official royal function and she'd enjoyed relaxing with the welcoming group.

'I wasn't very good at it but they were all eager for me to try.' There'd been laughter and encouragement and her participation had broken the ice. 'I did stumble a lot, not a good look in someone about to be Queen.'

Hessa would know the dance and probably perform it flawlessly.

'It wasn't about your competence.' Isam's mouth compressed. 'It was because the dance is one traditionally performed by young women before marriage. By virgins.'

Avril's eyes widened. She wasn't married yet and everybody knew she wasn't a virgin. 'But I was *invited* to dance with them.'

He nodded. 'Exactly. You did nothing wrong. Hafiz was trying to turn it into an insult. To say that the dance is only for sexually inexperienced women rather than simply for those about to marry. His statement reflected badly on him rather than you. As soon as he spoke out, pretending to be affronted, he was howled down.'

She digested that, forcing down distaste. 'And the incident in the market?'

Isam's pinched mouth and set jaw signalled discomfort. Or was that anger? 'He heard about your visit to the sweet shop and tried to turn it into something it wasn't.'

She thought over her visit to the vast covered market and the couple of minutes she'd spent in a delightful stall. The owner had invited her behind the counter so she could see how some of the delicacies were made and she'd left, smiling, with a box of tasty treats.

'I don't understand. I didn't do anything except taste some food. Shouldn't I have accepted the sweets?'

'As I said, you didn't do anything. It was just about you standing close to the stallholder.'

'But it was a tiny space.' Her eyes rounded. 'And we were in full view the whole time, apart from the counter between us and the rest of the market.' Her words tailed off as she read his expression. 'You're not serious! He thought the man hit on me?'

Isam looked uncomfortable. 'No, the opposite.'

Avril opened her mouth then closed it, words failing her. Eventually she managed, 'He accused me of what? Trying to seduce the guy?'

She shot to her feet and stalked across the room, arms wrapped around her middle.

'I told you it was nonsense. It's not about anything you've done or could do better.'

'No,' she croaked from a tight throat. 'It's about what I am. A scarlet woman, is that it? Because I had your baby.'

She turned to see Isam on his feet, concern pleating his forehead. He strode across to her, reaching for her hands but she whipped them behind her. She didn't want him to soothe her. She wanted, *needed* to know.

Isam froze as if she'd slapped him and instantly she regretted her action. But at the same time, she'd grown too used to being lulled by his reassurances.

'Tell me. *Please*, Isam.'

He shoved his hands in his trouser pockets, the action somehow making his straight shoulders seem even more powerful.

'You're right. Hafiz has tried to run that story. Since his attempts to disrupt my work haven't succeeded, he tried to blacken your character. But,' he continued when she would have protested, 'he hasn't succeeded. In fact his outlandish claims have rebounded. He's made himself a laughing stock and will soon lose what little support he thought he had. Everyone can see that you're not the sort of woman he claims. In fact, you're becoming very popular and admired.'

That might be true, yet Avril felt sick, nausea churning her stomach and her skin prickling hot then cold.

'Why didn't you *tell* me?'

'Because of exactly what's happening now. I wanted to avoid upsetting you. It was so patently untrue. No one believed his insinuations. Besides, Hafiz is about to abandon his political aspirations. You don't need to worry about him any more, Avril. I've seen to that.'

Avril frowned. That was good news but it didn't change the fact Isam had hidden the truth from her. 'I deserved to know!'

His steady gaze held hers. 'I apologise if you feel I've let you down. I didn't want to worry you. I put you in this position and I'm responsible.'

Her voice climbed an octave. 'Stop saying you're responsible for me. I'm responsible for myself!'

If he said it was his *duty* to protect her she might just scream. It was unreasonable but she'd come to hate that word.

Because she wanted to be so much more to him than a duty, someone he needed to protect.

Hurt as she was, it also pained her that the loathsome Hafiz used *her* to get at Isam.

'I know you're trying to do the right thing, Isam, but you're not helping. You're making this harder for me. I'm trying desperately to fit in but you won't trust me with the truth about things that concern me. You don't treat me as a real partner.'

His horrified look spoke volumes. 'You must know I trust you, Avril.'

Slowly she exhaled a shuddery breath. 'I do.'

Of course he trusted her. He was spending so much time helping her learn to act like a royal. That was his focus, securing his daughter by moulding Avril into a suitable queen.

Then she stunned herself as well as him by blurting out, 'But that's not enough.'

When they'd entered the room she'd felt a burst of exaltation, imagining he found her attractive in her new dress. But he'd just been thinking how her appearance would please his subjects, because she supported local industry.

He praised her often, but always about her ability to learn or her performance in public. All he cared about was her future public role. Her ability to undertake royal duties.

Isam said something but she didn't hear over the tumult in her blood.

Avril felt a ripping sensation inside, white-hot pain streaking through her then turning into a heavy anguished throb. As if some vital part of her had torn in two.

She stared into his stubbornly set features and confused eyes, and knew they could never go back to the way things had been.

This might have started with dismay at him keeping things from her. But now, suddenly, all the doubts and fears she'd battled for months coalesced, filling her with regret and resolution. And a terrible, terrible sadness.

Because finally she faced what she'd avoided ever since he'd proposed marriage.

'I can't do this any more, Isam. Coming here, living with you like this, was the biggest mistake of my life.' She sucked in air on a half-sob half-sigh, misery overflowing. 'I've tried so hard to convince myself, tried to believe we'd be happy and everything would work out for the best. But I can't marry you and be your queen. I just *can't*.'

Avril had spent so long pushing down her feelings, pretending it would be all right, that duty and a great sex life would be enough. And their shared love for Maryam.

Her eyes glazed so that when Isam towered over her, his

hands grasping her arms, she couldn't read his expression clearly. She blinked but her vision didn't clear.

'Tell me, Avril. Tell me everything.'

To her amazement, instead of anger, she thought she heard the deep resonance of concern in his voice.

That's what you want to hear. When will you stop fooling yourself?

His hold was supportive. That only made the pain well higher and faster, filling her till she didn't know what to do with it.

'Please, sweetheart. Talk to me.'

Something cracked inside her chest. When he used that endearment he almost undid her. It took her back to those intimate hours in his arms when they reached heaven together. When for a short time she'd believed the illusion that they were two halves of a single whole.

But it was an illusion. There was no romance, no love. There never would be. He used the endearment occasionally because he knew she liked it. That was all.

She told herself she was weak and selfish. She should put her daughter's needs above her own. But it did no good. Avril had reached the end. She couldn't go on.

'Please, Isam. I can't...' She swallowed, emotion thickening her throat. 'I can't do this now. I need to be alone.'

It was all she could do to stand there, blinking back the hot tears prickling her eyes, refusing to let them fall.

He said something she couldn't make out over her thundering pulse. When she didn't reply he finally let her go and stepped back.

It was a measure of her distress that his withdrawal made her want to cry out. Because despite her words, she wanted to be in his arms, wanted him to reassure her it would all be okay, though that was impossible.

She swung away from him, arms clutching tight around her middle, trying to hold herself together.

When he silently left the room, desolation engulfed her.

CHAPTER FOURTEEN

ISAM KNEW PAIN. Or thought he did.

He'd been to hell and back after the chopper accident.

He still missed his father every day. And though his memory had substantially returned, he was always aware of the gap around that fatal day and those last precious hours with his father.

For years he'd lived with guilt and grief over Nur's death.

But the despair he felt, having Avril tell him she'd tried but couldn't bring herself to marry him... That coming here and living with him was the biggest mistake of her life...

He felt undone.

Because *he* was the cause of her unhappiness.

He stared at the city view beyond his study window but saw instead Avril's face, pinched with pain.

How could it have come to this? He'd thought until recently that things were going so well. As they'd spent time together their relationship had blossomed. He could have sworn an intimacy was developing between them, ties that weren't related to their child or simple sexual attraction. The latter had always been phenomenal between them, yet that was only part of what he wanted with her.

In his youth he'd taken for granted the benefits of wealth, privilege and a physique that appealed to women.

He'd never met a woman horrified at the prospect of being with him.

He felt wrong in so many ways. Because Avril hadn't been annoyed or impatient. She'd been upset. More than that, distraught.

And in her pain she'd turned away from him!

He'd wanted to hold her to his heart and assure her they'd find a way through this.

All his life he'd believed he could deal with whatever he had to face. He knew deep inside that if everything else in his world was stripped away, he'd be content if he had Avril and Maryam. Once he'd have been amazed by that. He'd never expected to feel so deeply for a lover, had assumed that respect, liking and sexual compatibility would be enough to cement a marriage.

Now he saw he'd had no idea. His feelings for Avril, like those for his little daughter, ran as deep as the marrow in his bones, as strong as the fierce desert wind and as constant as the North Star.

But Avril didn't feel that way about him. He repelled her.

A dreadful plummeting sensation carved through his chest and belly, leaving him gutted.

He'd taken her for granted, assumed that because he wanted her, and it was logical for them to be together, he could make her happy.

He'd thought the worst he had to deal with was acclimatising her to her new role in his country.

It hadn't occurred to him that *he* wasn't enough for her.

A shudder began somewhere deep inside, growing in force until he had to plant his hand on the wall to keep his balance as the floor seemed to shift beneath him. Through his study window he saw the lights of the city dip and blur as if shaken by an earthquake.

But it wasn't the world that shook, it was Isam.

Reeling, he turned from the window and collapsed into the leather chair behind his desk.

He could insist. He could hold her to her promise.

If he wanted, he could force her to stay, blocking any exit from the country.

There had to be an argument he could make to persuade her to stay.

But then he remembered her torment. The anguish in her drowned eyes. The catch in her throat that spoke of despair and heartache.

Was he so arrogant he'd discount all that to get his own way?

Avril was many things. A tender mother. A passionate lover. An honest, dedicated worker. Someone who cared about others. Her joy in things like a picnic under the stars or learning a new language was a constant reminder that it was the simple things in life that made it worth living. Not the pomp and power. But the smiles and warmth.

Could he risk forcing her to stay and losing that for ever?

He braced his elbows on the desk, his head sinking into his hands.

He could have her by his side if he was ruthless enough. But at what cost?

It was hours later when Avril began to worry.

She'd fed Maryam and got her back to sleep. She'd paced and fretted and tried to talk herself into accepting the world Isam offered her. She'd tried to imagine herself flying back to London, returning to the little house she'd shared with Cilla. Tried to imagine her and Maryam there.

Tried to imagine life without Isam.

Her current situation was unworkable but she couldn't imagine a future without him. Where did that leave her?

The antique clock in the sitting room struck two and she realised how many hours had passed since Isam had left.

It was stupid to worry that he hadn't returned.

Why would he? He wouldn't choose to spend the night in her bed. He had a palace full of sumptuous bedrooms to choose from. She was the last person he'd want to see.

But he was always here to settle Maryam for the night after her last feed.

And he had so much riding on their marriage, Avril knew he wouldn't take her rejection at face value. He'd want to discuss it, try to persuade her to stay.

And…ridiculous as it was, she missed him. He was the one she needed to escape yet at the same time she craved the comfort of his arms about her, the sense she had when he held her that everything would work out well.

She ran her hands up and down her arms, trying to rub in some warmth.

Wait till the morning. Talk to him then, sensibly and calmly.

That was the logical thing to do. Except she remembered how he'd looked as she unravelled before him, almost incoherent, saying she couldn't stay and needed to be alone.

He'd been utterly shocked, her rejection coming out of the blue. She'd told herself she couldn't read his expression because of the tears blurring her eyes, but her conscience said otherwise. It told her he wasn't just surprised but grievously hurt.

She couldn't wait until tomorrow. She couldn't leave him hanging simply because she craved solitude. Isam deserved better.

Avril found him in his study. Seeing the light under the

door, she didn't knock but gently turned the handle and let herself in. Isam sat behind his desk, shoulders hunched as he looked down at a paper in his hand.

She paused just inside the door, drinking him in, wondering if this would be the last time she'd see him. That made her gasp, palm pressing to her aching chest.

'Avril.'

From under dark, straight eyebrows, cloudy grey eyes met hers. Her heart gave that familiar bump before quickening. But this time there was something else too, a stark pain of loss that echoed through every part of her body.

Even though she hadn't left yet.

For the first time she could recall, Isam didn't get up and come to her or invite her to sit. He simply stayed where he was, staring. Once she might have imagined his look was avid, as if eating up the sight of her. But that wasn't possible after what she'd said.

She told herself she was doing the right thing, ending this now rather than later. Yet it didn't feel right.

Legs shaking, she crossed to the desk, hyperconscious of the elegant green silk dress swishing around her legs. She didn't feel chic, she felt drab and heartsore as she sank into the chair in front of his desk.

Close up, he looked older, lines she hadn't noticed carving around his mouth and eyes. The scarring at his temple looked more livid and his mouth flatlined.

Was he angry or just disappointed?

He had to be both. After all he'd gone through with his amnesia and Hafiz, he didn't need this complication.

'I'm sorry, Isam. I should have told you much earlier. I should never have agreed to marry you.' She hitched a shallow breath. 'Hafiz will use this against you, won't he?'

She faltered to a stop, imagining the fallout of cancelling a royal wedding.

Isam had worked so hard to shore up his position after the trauma of the accident. If they separated there'd be a huge scandal. She'd played into Hafiz's hands.

'Don't worry about him.'

'But I do—'

'I told you. Hafiz is a spent force. Once we identified his spy in the palace we were able to catch him red-handed trying to sabotage not only me but senior members of the government. He's just confessed everything in a formal interview. The transcript of that tape will be shared with members of the Royal Council tomorrow. That's when I was going to tell you, as soon as it was over.' He paused then seemed to force himself to go on. 'The council will need to discuss it but Hafiz's bid for power is finished. Too many influential people will know about his underhand ways.'

Avril slumped back in her seat, relief filling her. If by her actions Hafiz had been able to wheedle his way onto the throne she'd never have forgiven herself.

But there was no relief from the pain she saw ahead, the pain even now racking her body. She bowed her head, staring at her tightly clasped hands, wishing there were some easy way out of this.

'Are you really so unhappy, Avril?'

Her vision blurred and she blinked, refusing to let the tears come. She nodded.

'Is there nothing I can say to persuade you to give us another chance?'

The breath caught in her throat as she heard tenderness and pain in that warm baritone voice.

He was a good man, a wonderful man, trying to do his

best for his daughter, his country and even her. It wasn't his fault he didn't love her.

Avril moistened her lips and swallowed hard, tempted to tell him there was one thing that would change her mind. But she'd never hear those words from him. He'd make a loyal and dutiful husband, but that was all. She'd never be the light of his life.

She cleared her throat. 'I'm sorry,' she whispered.

At least, she realised, this wouldn't be goodbye for ever. He wanted an integral role in Maryam's life. The obvious answer was for Avril to move with her somewhere close. It would be tough living in Zahdar without Isam, but her fantasy of returning to London was just that. Their daughter deserved both her parents and Avril had too much experience of parental neglect to deprive her.

That was the answer. A home in Zahdar's capital, or a smaller town along the coast a little where Avril wouldn't have to look up and see the palace every day.

That was an option at least for the first few years, so father and daughter could bond. After that maybe she'd return to London, with Maryam visiting her father for holidays.

Surely, Avril thought desperately, they'd find some workable arrangement.

The sound of Isam's chair being shoved back from the desk made her stiffen. He wasn't going to try to tempt her into changing her mind, was he? She knew what she needed to do but seriously doubted her ability to withstand Isam's kisses, even now.

Her head snapped up.

But instead of circling the desk towards her, Isam stalked to the window, staring out into the night, a crumpled paper falling from his hand. He shoved his hands in his trouser pockets, the action drawing the fabric tight across his firm buttocks, making her drag in an unsteady breath. She was still vulnerable to his potent attractiveness. She guessed that would never change.

Avril saw him in profile, proud, almost austere with his rigid posture and tight jaw.

'Very well.' His voice was gravel, scouring her flesh and her aching heart. 'I won't try to change your mind.'

His chin lifted and she saw his throat move convulsively. In this light he looked powerful, almost arrogant, yet that movement betrayed vulnerability. Pain bloomed. Not for herself but for Isam.

'I've been thinking,' she began, but he cut her off.

'You don't have to worry. I'll arrange everything. The announcement, the travel. But it may be better to wait a day or two before you and Maryam return to London. That will give my team time to sort out the security logistics, not just for your travel but longer term.'

Avril frowned. 'Longer term?'

Isam nodded, the movement brisk. But he kept his gaze fixed on the view beyond the window, as if he preferred not to see her.

'If you and Maryam are going to live in London I want to make sure you're safe. Let us do a security audit. In fact, it would be better if you let me buy you another house, one that's more private. Meanwhile you can stay in my London hotel suite.'

Avril swayed, momentarily unsteady, and had to reach for the desk to keep her balance.

He was agreeing to let her take their daughter away? To raise her in England?

'But if I take her to the UK you won't see her often.'

She saw him flinch, shoulders rising high under that dark jacket before he pushed them back down.

'I'll visit her when I can.'

The silence following his words made Avril feel empty inside. She knew what Isam's schedule was like. He tried hard to carve out time for them every day. But to visit London? Such visits would be rare.

'You wanted to be a hands-on father,' she whispered, feeling her insides turn over in a sickening tumble of distress.

This time he didn't flinch, just stared at the distant city streetlights. Was he thinking of the millions of people out there who looked up to him as their leader? 'We can't always have everything we want. I'll have to try to make it up to her when she's older.'

Avril put her hand to her mouth, stifling a cry of horror. That was one of the saddest things she'd ever heard. She knew how Isam loved their daughter. He positively revelled in being a father. For him family came first.

Was that why he was letting them go? Did he think Maryam would fare better if Avril was happy?

Isam was sacrificing his own bond with their daughter and it made Avril ashamed. She'd tried to make Maryam's need to be with both parents a priority, but when it came to the crunch she hadn't been able to go through with a loveless marriage.

Avril found herself circling the table, drawn to the pain radiating from the big man at the window. Hating that she was the cause. Wishing there were a better way for all of them.

Something crackled under her foot and she looked down to see the paper he'd been reading. Except he hadn't been reading. There was no text on it. Instead it was a large photo. She scooped it up.

Her heart beat louder and something snagged high in her

throat. It was one of the photos taken on the day their engagement was announced but she'd never seen it before. It
certainly hadn't been released to the public. It showed her
and Isam sitting together with Maryam. Avril was smiling down at their daughter but Isam wasn't. Nor was he
looking at the camera. His head was turned to Avril, his
expression unguarded.

She told herself the camera lied, that it was the angle or
the light making it look like something it wasn't.

Yet something leapt inside her. Something bright and
hopeful. His expression as he looked at her was familiar.
Not because she'd seen it before but because it was how
she felt about him.

She trembled and the photo fell from her unsteady hands.

'It's late. Go to bed, Avril. We'll talk when the sun's up.'

Still he didn't turn. Because he'd washed his hands of
her? Was he already planning his future without her? She
didn't believe it.

Avril moved closer until she stood just behind him, near
enough to inhale the comforting scent of citrus and warm
man. 'You're not going to try to persuade me to stay?'

Suddenly he was facing her, his grim face just above
hers. This close the pain in his eyes made her want to cry.

'You said there's no point and you wouldn't lie about
that. You're not that cruel.' Yet as he looked down at her
his eyes widened. What did he see in her face? 'Avril?'

Her heart pounded and she felt something like the mix
of fearful exhilaration she'd experienced the first time she
drove a four-wheel drive on a mountain road.

'But maybe I was mistaken,' she murmured. 'I was so
sure...'

Warmth enveloped her shaking hands. She looked down
to see Isam holding them tight.

'What were you sure about, sweetheart?'

Her heart dipped and soared. 'That you only wanted me for Maryam's sake. And to avoid scandal.'

Those long fingers tightened around hers. The blood beat through her body again and again as silence grew.

'That's what I thought, in the beginning.'

Avril's gaze flew to his. Her mouth dried at what she saw there.

'You must remember, I was raised expecting to contract a marriage of convenience. My family never married for love.' As if anticipating her interruption he shook his head. 'My grandparents were the sole exception to that and I know my grandmother missed my grandfather every day after his early death. If anything, that warned me off the idea of romance.'

He breathed deep, his chest rising. 'But that's not how I feel now. Now I understand exactly how my grandmother felt. These last months have been—'

'Wonderful,' Avril murmured, hardly daring to hope. 'More wonderful than I could have imagined.'

Isam's hands firmed around hers. 'But then that changed.'

She nodded. 'I told myself I could marry you and be happy for Maryam's sake. But every time we drew closer, something would happen to remind me our relationship is all about duty.'

'Avril, I—'

She interrupted, needing to explain, knowing he deserved the absolute truth, not just a snippet of it. 'Sometimes I hoped you might begin to love me just a fraction of the way you love Maryam.' Her voice wobbled. 'Because I love you. I think I always have. But all your praise was for when I did a good job, learning quickly or behaving the right way at an official function. It felt like your approval was never just for *me*.'

She hurried on when he would have interrupted. 'I *understand*, Isam. I know nothing is more important to you than Zahdar. That's always been your absolute priority. But you never saw me as a real *partner*. You were too busy protecting me. It didn't feel like trust or partnership, much less love.'

'And you deserve love.' His piercing eyes held hers and she felt the weight pressing down on her chest lift as he smiled. *'That's* what's been holding us apart. That's why you couldn't go through with our marriage.'

He was smiling now, his expression tender, and Avril was shaking so much he had to wrap his arms around her to support her, drawing her close.

Or maybe there was another reason for his action, because he needed her as much as she did him.

She looked up into his proud, dear face and warmth flooded her. The warmth of love and belonging.

'You were wrong about me not caring, Avril—'

'I know. I realised when you started planning to send me and Maryam back to London, and without a word of complaint. Even knowing the enormous scandal you'd face. You put my happiness above your own interests and desires.' Avril clutched his shoulders.

Isam met her stare with a look she'd never seen before. 'I'd sacrifice all I have, if it meant having you, Avril. You say nothing is more important to me than Zahdar, but if—'

She pressed a hand to his lips. 'Don't say it, Isam. I would never ask that.'

The thought of him giving up the role he'd spent his life preparing for didn't bear thinking about. He wasn't just devoted to his country, he was excellent as its leader and his people loved him.

Isam pressed a kiss to her fingers then drew her hand away, planting it over his chest so she felt his powerful heartbeat.

'I love you, Avril.' His words made the world still and all her senses heighten. 'In a different way but just as strongly as I love our daughter. I want you to be happy more than anything. Because I love you with all my heart.'

She stared in awe, everything inside her jangling in delight. 'That's why you agreed to let me leave?'

'What else could I do? You tried your best to fit in here, I knew that. And if you weren't going to be happy here I had no alternative.'

'It wasn't the place that was the problem, Isam.'

'It was me.' He drew a deep breath, his chest rising beneath her palm. 'If only I'd known. I was attracted to you right from the first. That night in London I knew you were out of bounds but I just couldn't resist. None of the arguments in my head could deter me.'

'You remember that?'

His mouth curved into a crooked, endearing smile that she felt deep in her core. 'I remember it all now, every glorious detail. In fact, it was seeing you again across the conference table that ignited my memories. That's why I had to leave you with my staff. I was getting flashbacks, of very intimate moments.' His chuckle delighted her and she found herself smiling back. 'I tortured myself for ages, believing I'd seduced you.'

'And now you remember how it really was. That I was responsible.'

'It was mutual. We were both responsible.' Isam shook his head as he hugged her to him. 'I took a long time, realising exactly how I felt about you. It was only tonight, at the prospect of losing you, that I found a name for it. I've broken with family tradition and fallen in love, Avril.'

She laughed breathlessly. 'Your grandparents would be proud of you.'

'I think you're right.' He paused. 'I confess I've spent a lifetime learning to shoulder responsibility and protect others. In theory those are fine traits but you've taught me they need to be tempered.'

His arm tightened around her waist and he drew himself up. 'If I promise to share more with you, rather than assuming I need to take charge, will you reconsider and stay?'

'Don't, Isam! Of course I'll stay. I love you. Don't make this sound like it was all your fault. It's mine too. I accused you of not sharing but I didn't either. I hoarded my feelings to myself, too scared to talk about them, because I've spent too long thinking myself unlovable. If I'd spoken out—'

'Shh.' Isam's lips grazed hers and nothing had ever felt so good. For she tasted understanding, love, and her own hopes for the future there. 'Let's agree that we both made mistakes and we'll trust each other with the truth from now on.'

Avril wrapped her arms around his neck and smiled with all the joy in her heart. 'That sounds absolutely perfect, my love.'

EPILOGUE

'YAY!' SHAKIL BOUNCED in his seat, clapping.

Beside him, Isam smiled indulgently. Over his son's head he caught Avril's gaze. Laughter lurked in those golden-brown depths.

'I know it's not approved royal behaviour,' Isam murmured as their son jumped to his feet in the grandstand, still applauding. 'But he's young and excited for Maryam.'

He was determined the children's education in royal behaviour would be tempered with the fun of simply being children. He wanted them to have balance in their lives as he now did. Thanks to his beloved wife.

Shakil loved football and couldn't wait to go to school next year and join the local schools' football competition. To him, having his older sister's team win their grade competition was the next best thing.

Beside Shakil, his twin, Sara, applauded just as enthusiastically. But Isam knew that when they returned to the palace, instead of picking up a football or basketball, she'd curl up with a picture book or draw today's events with her prized new coloured pencils.

He and Avril were blessed with children who were all fascinating individuals. He wondered what the future would bring them and knew that, whatever it held, there'd be an abundance of love.

'What are you thinking, Isam?' Avril had risen to her feet and paused beside him.

Isam rose, catching her hand in his and drawing her closer. Inevitably there'd be cameras trained on them but by now Zahdaris were accustomed to seeing signs of affection between their sheikh and sheikha. The friends and VIPs sitting around them didn't even turn to look.

'I'm thinking how very lucky I am to share this with you, sweetheart.' His gesture encompassed the children beside them and their older daughter down on the football field, lined up with all the others who had participated in the schools' competition. His words were pitched for Avril's ears alone. 'You make me whole.'

She stood there, in her dress of amber silk, wearing the heirloom ring he'd given her and matching ruby earrings. But it wasn't what she wore that made her gorgeous, it was her inner beauty and the light of love in her eyes.

Suddenly he became aware of the silence around them as the crowd waited for the VIPs to reach the microphone and begin the presentations.

His wife blinked, eyes bright. 'You do pick your moments, Your Majesty. But just so you know, I feel exactly the same.' She leaned in and whispered in his ear. 'Let's continue this discussion when we're home and the children are asleep.'

Isam squeezed her hand then released it, feeling the zing of anticipation low in his body.

He sat down and watched as Avril made her way to the podium where she and one of Zahdar's most internationally successful athletes would begin the presentations.

Applause swirled around the stands. For the children on

the field and for the two women on the podium who were both crowd favourites.

Sara came and sat on his knee to get a better view. Shakil climbed onto his other leg and Isam cuddled them both close. Then he lifted his gaze to his beloved wife, his smile full of pride and love.

* * * * *

If you just couldn't put down
Unknown Royal Baby,
then you're certain to love these
other emotional stories by Annie West!

The Housekeeper and the Brooding Billionaire
Nine Months to Save Their Marriage
His Last-Minute Desert Queen
A Pregnancy Bombshell to Bind Them
Signed, Sealed, Married

Available now!

HARLEQUIN
Reader Service

Enjoyed your book?

Try the perfect subscription for Romance readers and get more great books like this delivered right to your door.

See why over 10+ million readers have tried Harlequin Reader Service.

Start with a Free Welcome Collection with free books and a gift—valued over $20.

Choose any series in print or ebook. See website for details and order today:

TryReaderService.com/subscriptions